THE CALL HOUSE

A Washington Novel

C.P. STILES

Disclaimer

Dear Readers:

This story is based on actual events that took place in Washington, DC, during the early 1940s. All the names have been changed; most of the incidents have been invented; all of the conversations have been imagined.

It is not my intention to glamorize or romanticize prostitution—the women who ran this particular call house did try to protect the other women who worked there.

Please understand the portrayals of the DC police and the FBI are meant in fun. Both are more competent and less sinister. Most of the time.

Published in the United States by Bacon Press Books, Washington, DC www.baconpressbooks.com

Cover Design: Alan Pranke www.amp13.com

Editing: Lorraine Fico-White http://magnificomanuscripts.com

Book layout by ebooklaunch.com

ISBN: 978-0-9971489-4-7

For my family - for their patience

TABLE OF CONTENTS

I. February 1941 9

II. March 1941 33

III. April 1941 65

IV. July 1941 95

V. Summer/Fall 1941 125

VI. Winter/Spring 1942 157

VII. November 1945 183

THE CALL HOUSE

A Washington Novel

"Washington more than any other city in the world swarms with simpleminded exhibitions of human nature; men and women curiously out of place, whom it would be cruel to ridicule and ridiculous to weep over. The sadder exhibitions are fortunately seldom seen by respectable people; only the little social accidents come under their eyes."

Henry Adams
Democracy, An American Novel

I.

FEBRUARY 1941

1.

THE war changed everything. But that was later.

This was February 1941, and Washington had yet to become the city it was meant to be. Nation's capital? World capital? If you'd visited Paris or London, if you'd been to Boston or New York, then you knew Washington was still a small Southern town. Provincial and unsophisticated.

But if you were elected to Congress from Muskegon, Michigan, or Carbondale, Illinois, if you came looking for work from Greensboro, North Carolina, or Smyrna, Tennessee—Washington was the biggest goddamn city in the world. A Mecca for men of ambition. A refuge for women who refused to marry. And the closest thing to the Promised Land for anyone out of a job.

Ambitious and earnest, unmarried and adventurous, people poured in on trains and buses, crowding each other out of rooms in rundown boarding houses and bumping up against one another at night in the smoky bars on Capitol Hill or down on F Street where Negroes weren't allowed to take a seat unless they could play the piano.

It was February 1941—boys were men, women were girls, and everyone was more innocent than they'd ever be again.

But Mattie Simon didn't know any of that when she stepped off the train in Union Station, wearing a navy poplin shirtwaist dress with a white collar and matching navy-blue pumps. She carried a smooth cardboard suitcase tied together with rough twine.

All Mattie knew was she wanted adventure and her hometown didn't have any. She'd been bored with Smyrna as far back as third grade.

She had forty-seven dollars in a white handkerchief pinned inside her slip, and the addresses and phone numbers for the Red Cross and the YWCA tucked inside her purse. But somewhere on the train ride up she lost her nerve. In town ten minutes and already she was homesick. It wasn't at all what she imagined.

The vast marble and granite station was cold and crowded with men in heavy overcoats and broad-brimmed hats, women in dark tight-fitting suits and high-heels, sailors and soldiers and cops all in uniforms of their own. Mattie shielded her eyes against the late afternoon sun and tried to get her bearings, but the crowd pushed her along toward the exit. She felt her right ankle turn funny. She lost her balance.

Before she fell flat on her face, a sailor grabbed her by the arm.

"Good thing I was here to save you, sweet stuff." He was short and red-faced, with mean little eyes.

"Thank you." She smelled liquor and peppermint, cheap cologne, and hair pomade.

"You really want to thank me, baby doll, you can let me buy you a drink."

"Wish I could," she said, "But I'm . . ."

"Scared?"

Well, it turned out she was.

"Just not interested. I've got a fella back home." And wouldn't her momma have been happy if it had been true.

"And I've got a girl in sixteen ports. But right now, baby doll, all we've got is each other." He tightened his grip on Mattie's arm. She tried to pull away.

"Maybe you didn't understand me. I just want to show you a good time."

In the back seat of the sleek black sedan circling Union Station, Flo Maxwell leaned forward. She tapped her driver on the shoulder.

"Sam, did you see that? A striking girl in an awful blue dress. Looks like she could use some help. Circle again."

"Will do," Sam said. "But there's a cop on the corner hoping for trouble. Be careful."

The sailor pressed his body against Mattie's as they waited for a break in the traffic. She wriggled away.

"Easy now, you don't want to make a fuss. I'm just going to take you across the street to meet my buddies. Bet you never heard of a joyride where you came from."

The sleek black sedan stopped right in front of them. Air horns blared as Flo stepped out of the car. She wore a fur coat dark as the waters of the Potomac River. Her hair was the color of coal, her lipstick so red it made her teeth sparkle impossibly white. She walked right up to Mattie.

"There you are, darling. I've been looking all over for you," she said loud enough for the cop to hear. She towered over the sailor.

"What the—"

She pushed him aside and gave Mattie a hug.

"Why I was worried half to death I'd missed you, and here you were all along."

"Here I am." Mattie was still shaking.

"Look at you, you're shivering. I could have sworn I told your momma to make sure you packed a heavy coat. Never mind. Let's get you home." She put her arm around Mattie and steered her toward the car.

"Hey, what about me?" the sailor called after them. "Don't I get some kind of reward? I'm the one who found her."

"Keep walking," Flo said.

Sam held open the door to the sedan. He took Mattie's cardboard suitcase, handling it as carefully as if it were real leather, and put it on the front seat. He waited until Mattie settled herself in back, then closed the door.

"Thank you," Mattie said. "I swear I think you saved my life."

"Hush, honey. No one's going to hurt you while I'm around. New to town?"

Mattie straightened her collar, smoothed her skirt. "Does it show that much?"

Flo sat back and took stock. The clothes were dreadful, but she'd seen worse. Slim ankles, shapely legs, a trim waist. Could anyone tell what was hidden beneath her boxy poplin dress? A long graceful neck. A nearly perfectly heart-shaped face. And wasn't there just a hint of mischief behind those wide hazel eyes? A touch of naughty mixed in with all that nice?

"If I had to bet money," Flo said, "I'd bet you'll look like you've lived here your whole life in no time."

Mattie smiled—that was just what she wanted to hear.

"Sam, I'm guessing this young lady is headed over to the YWCA. Let's swing past there and drop her off."

"Sure thing." Sam caught Flo's eye in the mirror. "Hope she's got a reservation. You know they've been turning people away these past few months."

"Reservation? I didn't know I needed one." Mattie fumbled in her purse for the slip of paper. "All I've got is their address and phone number."

"Tell you what." Flo removed one of her long black leather gloves and patted Mattie's hand. "Why don't you come on home with me tonight? I've got an extra room."

"I hate to trouble you."

"No trouble at all."

Flo studied her again. Mattie had one of those smiles that lit up her face with a lifetime of secret hopes.

"Just sit back and relax," Flo said. "Everything will be fine now."

2.

IN the mornings, the bathroom was crowded with the sweet smells of lavender soap, gardenia perfume, and lilac dusting powder, with the bright colors of pink-red lipsticks and near-orange rouge, with drying stockings and still damp lingerie. With five women in one apartment, even an apartment as grand as Flo's on the top floor of the building on Connecticut Avenue, mornings were hectic.

Awake early but unsure what to do, Mattie ended up being last in line for the bathroom. She wasn't used to waiting.

She'd grown up with only her mother; her father had been wounded in the last war, his lungs badly damaged by gas. She barely remembered the man who died when she was four, but his absence lingered in the white clapboard house. Upstairs, her mother kept always to one side of the bed and lived so quietly, Mattie almost felt as if she'd grown up on her own.

A tall girl, with soft ash-blond curls, walked past Mattie waiting in the hall.

"You'll have to learn to be pretty fast around here if you want to get in the shower while we've still got hot water."

"That's all right," Mattie said. She'd never showered in hot water back home. Her momma hadn't wanted to trouble anyone to fix the water heater after it broke. She didn't like troubling anyone for anything, so when something broke, and it couldn't be fixed by prayer, it stayed broken. Mattie thought her momma's whole life stayed broken after her daddy died.

"I'll show you how it's done," the tall girl said.

She banged on the bathroom door. "Vera, there's exactly one of those jelly donuts left. If you want it, you'd better come grab it fast." She had to step back, the door opened so quickly.

"If you're lying to me, Charlotte, I'll kill you." Vera, wrapped in a peach silk robe, tied the belt tight around her tiny waist. Mattie thought it could have been Jean Arthur rushing past them to the dining room.

Charlotte held the bathroom door open for Mattie. "It's all yours. See you at breakfast."

The air in the bathroom felt close and warm, smelled exotic. Mattie gazed at herself in the gilt-edged mirror, steamed over and streaked. She touched the black-and-white flocked wallpaper that looked as if it were made of velvet. Stepping out of her slippers, she rubbed her bare feet on the smooth black-and-white marble floor. She turned the brass faucets shaped like fish, and water poured from their open mouths. Then she took the first hot shower of her life.

In the main dining room, Flo told everyone about Mattie before Mattie appeared, showered and powdered, the only one dressed in her good clothes—everyone else still in their silk robes, their satin pajamas, their heads wrapped in terry cloth turbans.

"Well, here she is," Flo said. "Mattie Simon, straight off the train from Alabama."

"It's really Tennessee," Mattie said.

"Kid," Charlotte touched Mattie's arm, "everyone is from someplace else. And it doesn't matter where. All that counts is you're here now. And we've still got one jelly donut left."

Charlotte moved her chair so Mattie could sit down at the place next to hers and passed along a silver platter splattered white with powdered sugar, a fat donut leaking red raspberry jelly balanced right in the middle.

Flo cleared her throat. "Evelyn will give you your schedules for today. Anyone's got free time, let me know. We've got something special coming up for tomorrow night."

A small, elegant woman with shiny ginger-colored hair and dark eyes passed out cards. "Now that Congress is back," Evelyn said, "we're going to be pretty busy."

"All this war talk means an awful lot of meetings in the next few months," Flo said. "Don't skimp on your beauty sleep, take your vitamins, get plenty of fresh air. We can't afford to have anyone out sick."

Charlotte looked at the card Evelyn gave her and started coughing. "Talk about getting sick," she said, coughing harder. "I think you'd better cancel my three o'clock. I must be coming down with something."

Vera grabbed the card away from Charlotte and read it. "Looks like she's got a bad case of Spencer Voorhees." Everyone around the table laughed.

"I can get Doc to give you some cod liver oil," Flo said.

Charlotte made a face, tucked the card in her pocket. "You'll catch on soon," she whispered to Mattie.

"Mattie, honey," Flo said, as the others folded their linen napkins, pushed back their chairs. "Why don't you come and talk to Evelyn and me. You're probably going to be looking for work. I think maybe we can help."

3.

"YOU know I'd trust you with my life," Evelyn said. "You've got more business sense than any ten men. But I still don't know what you see in this new girl."

They were having one of their rare dinners away from the Franklin Institute at Ciro's Italian Village on G Street. No one they knew ever ate there—it was safe. They could talk freely, eat and drink as much as they wanted.

"The girl has no experience. I'd bet she's never been to any place as sophisticated as a Hot Shoppes. She's no match for the smooth-talking men in this town. We'd be doing her a favor to let her go before she gets into trouble."

Flo nearly drowned her iceberg lettuce in olive oil, went light on the vinegar. The taste took her back to the one summer she spent in Florence with her family when she was fifteen. She tore through a plate of ravioli. She hadn't been home in two years.

"You're not telling me anything I don't know. I still think she's got something. She's bright. She's curious. She came here alone—we both know that takes guts." Flo broke off a piece of Italian bread and mopped up the tomato sauce still left on her plate. "Right now, she's trying to figure out how to shed her old skin and step into a new life. She's a little scared, but give her time. She'll get there. She reminds me of us when we first came to town."

"That's what I'm afraid of. Even money says she'll fall in love with the first man who pays any attention."

Flo put down her fork. They had an unspoken agreement to leave the painful past right where it belonged—behind them. Flo never mentioned Sherman, though she still wore the locket he gave her the night he confessed he was married. Someday, he promised, they'd find a way to be together. No reason to wait for him but no reason to throw out a necklace that nestled so nicely in that soft spot on her neck.

And Evelyn never said a word about Randall—her childhood sweetheart who proposed at their high school prom. Everyone saw him get down on one knee on the dance floor. Two months later, everyone saw Randall and Coretta Springer kissing in the movie theater balcony—no one told Evelyn until a week before the wedding.

By choice and circumstance, Flo and Evelyn never talked about men except as clients. They didn't date. Who had the time? They were too busy running a business, keeping everyone happy. At the end of each day, Flo liked nothing better than to slip underneath her satin sheets with a good book and a glass of cold white wine. Evelyn, in her flannel nightgown, would listen to the radio before she fell asleep. As long as the cops didn't bother them, this was their present and future.

The candle in the Chianti bottle dripped wax onto the red-and-white checkered tablecloth. Flo scraped it off with one of her long red fingernails.

"I've got a hunch Mattie's tougher than we think. Let's keep an eye on her. Give her another month," Flo said.

"Fine. But if she hasn't gotten over her jitters by then, we're going to need to find someone else. If it was up to you, we'd be taking in stray kittens and passing out soup. We can't afford it. Not now. Not a month from now. We've got to be careful."

4.

BETTY Prince gently tugged on the frayed cord from the Venetian blinds. If she pulled too hard, the blinds would slip off their brackets and crash to the floor, startling the Congressman awake. She only wanted to let in the sunlight, to let Congressman Stevens know his long night of working in his office was over. It was the third time this week she'd found him asleep on that cracked leather couch. He was working too hard.

Andrew Stevens kept his eyes shut against the sun. He could feel the stiffness in his neck from sleeping without a pillow. His legs felt tight from trying to fit his six-foot-two-inch frame onto a couch four inches too short. He could tell he needed a shower. But he wasn't ready to face the day and he wasn't ready for another one of Betty's lectures. She meant well, but the last thing he needed in Washington was another woman watching over him.

Too many of his colleagues' wives had already overwhelmed him with kindness. His small refrigerator held more casseroles, more congealing dishes of Welsh rarebit, than he could eat in a month. Plus, all the dinner invitations. Always to meet some eligible niece in town visiting. Some dear female friend.

The wives embarrassed him by saying they were sure he'd be one of the brightest stars in Congress. They insisted he needed a good woman behind him to help him get ahead. His own mother, back home in Michigan, wrote him weekly to say the same thing.

He tried to ignore them. He was determined to concentrate on the important work he'd been elected to undertake. How to feed and clothe and find jobs for the thousands of men still struggling to hold onto whatever gains they'd made since the Depression. Whether to ease this country into the war that increasingly seemed inevitable.

But bad luck latched onto him and wouldn't let go. Instead of getting one of the prized slots on the House Military Affairs Committee, as new man in town he was shunted off to the committee that handled oversight of the District of Columbia. A city he loathed.

Pain shot from his neck to his head. Since he'd been sleeping on his couch, he'd been having fierce headaches. Backaches. Pains in his arms and legs. He finally had to open his eyes.

Betty, in a blue-and-white polka-dot dress, her hair pulled back tight in a bun, shook her head. She played the part of mother hen so perfectly, Andrew was sure he could hear her clucking at him.

"The least you could do," Betty stood in front of him with her hands on her wide hips, "is tell them to give you a longer couch. A man your size shouldn't have to curl up like that when he wants to sleep." She always sounded angry when she was trying to be kind.

"Is there time for me to catch a shower?"

She opened the thick leather appointment book. Andrew knew she memorized every appointment. He was beginning to understand she lived his life as if it were her own but liked to pretend she didn't.

"Sorry, boss. All you've got time for is a quick shave. And if you'd remembered to keep an extra shirt and tie here, you could stand a change of clothing. You've got the District Committee at nine and Spencer Voorhees for lunch at noon."

Andrew made a face. He'd been trying to avoid Voorhees. A dreadful man with way too much power. But John Winston, the senior representative from Michigan, his colleague, mentor, and just about his only friend in town, told Andrew to stay on Voorhees's good side. Far as Andrew could tell, the man didn't have one.

Betty brought him coffee, light, one lump. She pushed aside papers on his desk to make room. "If you had a wife, you'd have a reason to go home. Have a decent breakfast."

"Betty, what would I do with a wife when I've already got you? What more could I want for breakfast besides a cup of your coffee and the newspaper?"

But damn if the newspaper didn't have another one of those stories about rampant vice in the District of Columbia, the town he now had the responsibility of saving. Another police raid on the restrooms at Union Station, and seventeen sailors under arrest for indecent behavior. The chief of police and the head of the vice squad were calling on Congress to write laws with some teeth in them. *How can we fight a war overseas when our boys are dying of VD right at home?* they wanted to know.

He took two aspirins.

5.

IN Tom Callan's office at DC Police Headquarters, the small group of police officers who made up the District of Columbia's vice squad squeezed in knee-to-knee on wooden folding chairs facing a scratched oak desk. A yellowed shade, nailed to the only window, shut out the light. Callan, tall and thin, his face still scarred from a raging teenage acne, paced in front of his men. Some days his arthritis twisted his left hand so badly, it looked like a claw. He had a crudely fitted glass eye—the result of a knife fight, he told his men. Only his family knew how he accidentally burned himself with acid from his Chemcraft Junior chemistry set, trying to perform the kind of chemical magic lonely adolescents practiced in their basements.

"Have you seen the headlines?" he asked. Only one of the cops, Daniel Granger, his first week on the squad, nodded. The rest of the men knew Callan didn't want an answer.

Callan stopped in front of his desk, stared hard at his men with his one good eye. He picked up the newspaper and rattled it at them.

"Have you seen this? *VD Out of Control in DC,*" he read from the front page. "It says the District of Columbia has the highest rate of venereal disease of any city in this country. The highest rate." He walked over to the brass spittoon by the door and spat right into it.

He looked up and stared at his men again. "This place is turning into a cesspool. They're talking about making Washington off-limits to servicemen. And I say that can't come too soon." This time the men nodded.

"We've got more degenerates in sailor suits coming into this town on leave than any other place on this earth. But I don't have to go into details with you boys. You know what I'm talking about. That's why you've been handpicked for this job." He raised his twisted hand and scanned the room slowly to see if anyone dared smile.

"We can't afford to wait for a bunch of fat and lazy politicians to pass some ordinance while flagrant vice is killing this city. If we want something done—we've got to be the ones to do it. You got that?"

Daniel Granger couldn't keep from speaking out loud. "Yes, sir."

"What?" Callan turned to see which of his boys dared to speak.

The men on either side of Daniel inched their chairs away from him. They knew Callan was a man of many moods, most of them dark.

"Go on," Callan said, staring at Daniel.

"Right down the street from where my mother goes to church, I'm sure they're running a brothel in of one of those transient hotels. My own mother can't go to Mass on Sundays without passing an . . . um," he cleared his throat, "lady of the night. Pardon my French."

The other cops looked to see how Callan would take this interruption.

"Hey, blondie," the cop next to Daniel said, under his breath, "you're not in school any more. You don't get points for being teacher's pet."

Callan pretended he didn't hear the taunting. Do the kid some good to get roughed up a little. He never liked taking on those college boys, even the dropouts, but Daniel's uncles were on the force. They pleaded with Callan to give the kid a break—he passed the special training at the Police Academy while working two jobs and going to school. That kind of dedication had to count for something. He didn't tell the uncles he would have taken the kid no matter what—he was desperate for new recruits.

Chief Coker, the head of the Metropolitan Police and a man Callan never liked, warned him he'd lose his badge if DC didn't get cleaned up fast.

Coker gave him six months to rid the city of the pimps and the madams who met young girls at the train station and turned them right out on the street. To shut down the bar owners who still served moonshine in secret back rooms where men could gamble. To arrest the homosexuals who were more of a threat to this good American town than any ten communists right off the boat from Moscow.

If he could run them all out of town, he'd get his promotion. Otherwise, Coker warned him he'd be out on his keister.

"Son," Callan focused hard on Daniel, "if we had laws with some teeth in them, we'd go raid that place near your mother's church tonight. But right now, our hands are tied by those fat, lazy bastards in Congress who treat this town like their own personal plantation."

"Then what can we do, Sarge?"

"Well, I'm glad you asked." He walked around to the front of his desk, perched half on the edge. "First, we want to keep our eye on all those brothels and call houses, on all those sailors and sissy boys pouring in every day trying to ruin this city for the decent folk who live here. We want to watch, and we want to wait. And when the time is right, we want to catch those degenerates with their pants down."

6.

MATTIE had never done anything like this in her life. She wasn't sure she could go through with it. Her momma would never approve. Even Aunt Lil, the most sophisticated woman she'd known before she reached Washington, might look funny at the whole idea of walking into a department store and charging a new dress, hat, and shoes to a man she'd never met.

But Flo insisted she buy new clothes and charge them to someone named Frank. She said a young woman with Mattie's potential could not afford to hide her light under a bushel. And that navy-blue poplin dress was worse than a bushel. Flo said she'd give it to charity if Mattie would promise to pick up something a little more flattering. Ask for the saleswoman named Trix and she'd be sure to get the right help. At the last minute, Charlotte talked Flo into letting her go with Mattie to Garfinkel's Department Store on F Street.

Charlotte grabbed dresses off the rack so fast, Mattie didn't have a chance to look at them before Trix whisked them off to the dressing room.

"Hmm." Charlotte held an ice-blue chiffon dress under Mattie's chin. "The color is good with your eyes but you're a little short-waisted. You need something to make you look like you have a longer torso."

"Definitely," Trix said, draping a red satin dress across Mattie's shoulders. "I like red for her. Especially if it's for dinner at the Mayflower. The lighting there is heavenly for red. Get the Crab Bisque. The Lobster Thermidor. And promise me you will not leave until you've tried the Baked Alaska."

"Bananas Foster," Charlotte said. "Cherries Jubilee. If it doesn't come flaming to your table, you can't really consider it your first night on the town."

Flo mentioned dinner with some friends visiting from Detroit. Important, wealthy men who liked to be seen in the company of good-looking young women. That's how it was in Washington, Flo told her. Evelyn agreed. Charlotte made it unanimous. If Vera was too busy to go, Flo said she'd appreciate it if Mattie would do this one small favor for her.

"You have nothing to worry about," Flo said. "They're real gentlemen. Besides, Charlotte will be there to show you everything you need to know."

"Doesn't look like there's a whole lot I'll need to teach you," Charlotte said as Mattie modeled the red satin dress. "Don't know what you've been doing down in Alabama all these years, but kid, you're a natural."

Mattie twirled in the dress in front of Charlotte, in front of Trix, then alone in the dressing room in front of the three-way mirror. She felt like a movie star, like someone else entirely. It didn't feel wrong, but it didn't feel right, either.

"How are you doing in there?" Charlotte called through the dressing room curtains.

"Fine. I'm just trying to figure out how to get out of this dress. It seems there are an awful lot of strings attached."

"Strings?" Charlotte said.

"Like Frank. Why would he pay for all this when I've never even met him? It's a little too good to be true."

"You'll see. There's not one truly good thing about him."

"I knew it." Mattie started to unzip the dress. "I shouldn't be doing this."

"Kid, no reason to worry before you have to. Enjoy yourself tonight. Besides," Charlotte said, "how could you turn down a dress that looks like it was made for you?"

Mattie had to admit it did.

Charlotte picked out red satin pumps. Trix picked out a hat that was hardly a hat at all, just a strip of red satin held onto her head by combs. Charlotte would lend her a pair of red gloves and Flo had jewelry to spare.

"That pretty much covers it," Charlotte said. "You do know how to dance, don't you?"

But Mattie didn't. Her last boyfriend, Charlie, had two left feet, sweaty palms, and an aversion to dancing so intense, it gave him hives. She practiced secretly in her room, imagining Fred Astaire in place of Charlie, but she'd never danced out on a dance floor with a rich and important man holding her in his arms.

She never imagined she'd have to learn with tiny Vera as her partner in the sitting room back on Connecticut Avenue, spinning her around to Glenn Miller's "Moonlight Sonata" until she grew dizzy and giddy.

"Let him lead," Vera said. "Stare into his eyes, lean into his arms a little, and he'll think you're wonderful."

When Charlotte joined them, she curled up quietly in a corner of the sofa. She was back in her bathrobe, though it was only late afternoon. The sparkle gone from her green eyes, she looked pale.

"Are you okay?" Mattie said.

"Don't worry about me, kid. It's been a long day. Maybe I'll catch forty winks before we go out tonight. I think I've earned them."

"Isn't there something I can do?"

"Sure there is." Vera grabbed Mattie's hand to keep her from following after Charlotte. "You can learn the jitterbug so you don't go landing on someone else's feet." She opened the cover of the electric Victrola and put on "In the Mood."

7.

AT 1:00 a.m., when all the respectable residents of Washington were home in bed, Sergeant Callan lined up his men along the side of the Greyhound Bus Terminal, out of the way of travelers.

He'd received a tip some dime-store dames were operating in back of the terminal on New York Avenue. They picked up men in the Pink Elephant Lounge at the Harrington Hotel and sweet-talked those drunken dupes into taking a walk down the street. After doing their business up against the station wall, those babes would beg for a few extra bucks and catch the next bus out of town. But not tonight. Tonight, Callan would be there to catch them.

He alerted the papers—a raid like this was big news. He was sure that hack of a police-beat reporter Bud Rourke would show. Rourke would write any story as long as there was a bottle of Chivas Regal attached to it. He'd probably bring along his half-pint photographer, "Izzy" Israel. The pair was almost as bad as the city scum they covered.

He already warned Izzy about snapping him from the left side. That wasn't what he wanted to see on the front page of *The Times-Herald.*

Under the light of the street lamp, he checked his men. He made sure their shoes shone, their buttons gleamed, the creases in their trousers as sharp as the blade of the bone-handled knife he kept taped to his calf, and the visors on their caps clean enough to bounce the light. Daniel glistened like a Christmas ornament. Callan could see his own reflection in the tops of Daniel's shoes.

"You call that a shine?" He was harder on the kid than the rest of them because the boy had the most promise. "You get down there and shine them again." He needed to kill time anyway—Rourke and Izzy were running late.

Daniel hesitated.

Was the kid going to do it? Callan shook his head. "Forget it. I want all of you to wait right here until I give you the signal."

Callan stepped into the street to get a better view of the area. It was a cold clear night and he could see all the way down New York Avenue—quiet and empty. The weather must have kept the bums inside. He rubbed his hands together. On nights like this his bad hand twisted up so he couldn't uncurl his fingers.

"Hey, *Cullen*," Bud Rourke called as he rounded the corner at 11th Street, "you gonna stand there wringing your hands like an old lady or are you gonna give us the story you promised?" Rourke wore a knit cap, a heavy woolen coat, two scarves, and thick woolen mittens.

Callan looked at Rourke all bundled up. "Who's the old lady? Afraid of a little cold weather?"

"Could I be afraid of anything when I've got you and your boys keeping this city safe?"

"Make sure you get my name right. It's *Callan*, with an *A*."

Izzy Israel came chugging up 11th Street as fast as his short legs could carry him. He had a cigarette in his mouth and two Speed Graphics in a burlap sack hung around his neck. He slapped his arms at his sides to warm himself.

"Nothing better than a couple of hot dames to warm you up on a night like this," Izzy said.

"You gotta admire a man who likes his work," Rourke said to Callan.

Callan was tired of making nice to the press boys. He checked his watch; the paddy wagon would be there in ten minutes. More than enough time to surprise those dames and get them in handcuffs. "Listen up," he said to his men. "We're going to go to the back of this building. No rough stuff. Play it by the book."

The men nodded. They could tell Daniel was itching to ask what book, so they held him back.

He led his men around the side of the building. The air smelled of gasoline fumes and fresh tar, rotting garbage and cat piss. The acrid smoke burned his eyes.

Smoke? He drew his nightstick. Rourke pulled off his mittens with his teeth; he took out his notebook and pencil. Izzy put a new bulb in his flash.

"Police," Callan yelled. "Stop what you're doing and get your hands in the air."

He expected to catch half a dozen half-naked couples. Instead he found two bums crouched over a brush fire, hands in the air.

"Holy shit," one of the bums said looking up at the line of policemen coming his way.

The other bum stood, keeping his hands above his head. "It wasn't me, I swear. It was him." He dropped his right arm to point at his partner. "If you don't believe me, check inside his jacket."

The other bum opened his coat. Callan tightened his grip on his nightstick.

"Here," the bum said. "Take it, take all of it." He held out a can of baked beans, an onion, and a tin of sardines. "We was hungry. We didn't mean to steal."

Izzy, always a little quick on the trigger, took a picture of the bum handing over his can of baked beans.

Rourke, his pencil poised, looked at the police sergeant. "That's *Callan* with an *A*—right?"

8.

MOST of the seasoned, silver-haired congressmen Andrew met told him they left their offices by six at the latest. No reason to read through every single report—that's what their staff was for. He didn't have any staff besides Betty. He wouldn't have passed along his work to someone else anyway. But there was so much to read, he didn't have time for anything else. He turned down an invitation to dinner at the Mayflower with the visiting businessmen from Detroit. For the sake of his career, he should have gone. But how would he have any career at all if he spent every evening socializing?

"Ask me how I knew I'd find you here," Spencer Voorhees said, standing in the middle of the doorway to Andrew's office, bold as a bad dream.

Not for the first time, Andrew wondered why so many of these ancient congressmen and senators seemed to have such large heads. Heads too big for their scrawny old necks, crepey skin draping over their starched white collars.

He smiled at Spencer Voorhees. "I don't know, sir. You must have some sixth sense."

"Some people call it intuition."

Voorhees, with his heavy Southern accent, took one syllable and made it two, made "intuition" sound like something Andrew never heard of before.

"Plus, I have eyes and ears all over the House, all up and down the halls of the Senate. You don't believe me, boy, just try to get something past me and see if you can."

Andrew had heard all about Voorhees. The other freshman congressmen talked about nothing else. The rumor was Voorhees could make or break your career. If he ever showed up at your office, and rumor was he often did, it meant he wanted a favor you shouldn't refuse.

Voorhees treated Washington like his own private playground. He considered himself the unofficial mayor of the town. Never mind the three commissioners appointed by the president who were supposed to be in charge, Voorhees controlled the permits and the purse strings. Nothing could get built without his approval. Nothing could get done without his blessings. Voorhees and his friends, all reigning powers in Congress, could get more worked up about whether to build a bridge over Rock Creek Park, or another traffic circle near the District line than they did about the fall of Poland, Belgium, and France.

But that didn't stop him from itching to get into the war. Voorhees needed Andrew's support to extend the draft. He had been pursuing his new colleague for weeks. He sent Andrew invitations to parties, receptions, and private dinners.

Andrew turned them all down and kept his distance, but tonight's visit was waiting for him all along. No one seemed able to escape Voorhees's ham-handed clutches.

"Sorry I had to cancel our lunch," Voorhees said. "Thought maybe you and I could have ourselves a friendly cocktail before I head home to the missus."

"Thank you, sir. I'd be honored."

"You can cut the 'sir' crap. It's not going to do you any good. Either I like you or I don't. And right now, I'm not sure."

Andrew followed Voorhees back to the older man's office where Voorhees kept his bourbon, crystal highball glasses, and a full bucket of ice.

"I'm glad we finally have this chance to get to know each other." Voorhees motioned for Andrew to sit next to him on the dark brown leather sofa. "From what I've seen so far, and no disrespect intended, I believe there's a helluva lot I can teach you."

Voorhees unbuttoned his jacket. Andrew could see his red suspenders, decorated with bull dogs, stretched almost to breaking over his wide belly.

Voorhees raised his glass in salute then downed his bourbon so fast, he seemed to inhale it. "Now there's two things you need to know."

Andrew tried to strike a pose that would make him look wise beyond his years.

"You probably came here with all those nice ideals a fine young boy like you picks up out there in the Midwest. You probably heard how what we do here is compromise. Let me tell you first off, there's no such thing as compromise—there's only winning and losing. None of us likes it when we lose, so it gets harder to reach an agreement next time around. Which is why you've got to pick your fights. You've got to know when to go to the mat and when to hold back." Voorhees stopped to pour himself another drink.

"Lesson number two. This town is made up of two kinds of people. Half of 'em are Eagle Scouts, debate team winners, model citizens. The other half are conmen and horse traders. Wanna know which ones I trust? I'll take the horse traders every time. Can't count on an Eagle Scout to know which way is up without a compass. Civic-minded citizens'll be the death of this good country. A man's got to be practical if he wants to get ahead. The best piece of advice I can give you, son, is figure out who your friends are and stand by them. Loyalty. That's what makes you feel good in your gut."

With a hearty show of Southern friendship, Voorhees poked Andrew in the gut, then hit him on the back. Andrew cried out in pain.

"Can't take it, eh, boy?"

Andrew, usually so reluctant to discuss his personal problems, told Voorhees about his neck, the shooting pains in his jaw. If he were back in Muskegon, he would have gone to the chiropractor. Did Voorhees know of any?

"Chiropractor?" Voorhees laughed, reached out to give Andrew another one of those heavy-handed back slaps, then stopped himself. "You're in the city, now, boy. What you need to do is get yourself one of those *may-sah-ges.*"

Andrew thought he'd learned how to keep his ignorance from showing all over his face, but it must have been apparent he didn't know what Voorhees was talking about.

"Surely even a Midwestern boy like you knows what that is. They teach them over there in Sweden how to rub your back so hard and it hurts so good you don't ever want it to stop. I go every week. Get myself a nice steam bath. I've got just the place for you."

Voorhees gestured with his outsized hands so Andrew understood he was talking about a massage.

As far as Andrew knew they didn't have massages in Muskegon. He'd probably have to go all the way to Grand Rapids. Only he never would.

"Don't say no till you've tried it. A man can't work if he's distracted by pain. This is what we'll call a career move."

Andrew spent his first months learning the hard way that everyone spoke in code. The old horse traders in Congress never wanted to go on the record until they lined up the support they needed, so they spoke indirectly. With so many innuendoes and hints, sometimes threats, maybe bribes, he was sure he'd never figure it out without one of those decoders the army was working on. He did know this much, from the way

Voorhees looked at him, from the way he smiled—the man was clearly driving at something—Andrew wasn't sure what.

"You leave it all to me. I'll get my girl to make an appointment for you. You're going to thank me for this."

The last thing he wanted was to be indebted to Voorhees. From what he'd heard, he would never get free. It would make life on the District Committee even more difficult.

On the other hand, maybe he was being too cautious. Maybe all Voorhees was offering was some relief. His neck was driving him crazy. That healing balm Betty left him did nothing to relieve the sharp shooting pains.

His old girlfriend Lorraine told him he spent so much time looking at a subject from every single angle she half-expected to find him standing on his head once he got to Washington. From the way his head ached, Andrew was sure someone must have been standing on it.

9.

THE beauty salon in the Shoreham Hotel smelled of permanent wave lotion, nail polish, and sweet-scented hairspray. One woman in a pink uniform circled the chairs every ten minutes, sweeping shorn locks off the pink-tiled floor. Another woman in pink wheeled the coffee and pastry cart past the row of clients seated under the hair dryers.

Mattie didn't need to tell Flo she was unhappy with her hairstyle for Flo to make an appointment for her. Again, she insisted they would put it on Frank's tab. Mattie still didn't know who Frank was. Flo said they'd clear up that mystery over the weekend. Frank was coming to visit. Which was why it was especially important for Mattie to get her hair done. First impressions always count.

Flo played with Mattie's hair a little, pushing it this way, combing it that. "What do you think?" she asked Evelyn. "Linda Darnell or Rita Hayworth?"

"Definitely Rita Hayworth," Evelyn said. "She's got the height."

"Only not as red," Flo said. "Maybe auburn."

"Auburn?" Monsieur André sniffed when she repeated Flo's instructions. "That is totally out of the question. Not with your coloring."

He was clearly not happy with her. Not with her hair, which he held in his fingers. Not with her posture and the way she held her head—he kept placing his hands on her ears and tilting her head the way he wanted it, then grabbing her by the ears again and forcing her to tilt her head half an inch the other way. "Stay like that," he said, "otherwise it is utterly impossible for me to work."

She felt trapped under the rubberized pink cape they snapped over her shoulders. It pinched her neck. Water leaked down her back and her new blouse was damp. But she hadn't wanted to change out of her clothes. Back home, Aunt Lil always did her hair. They kept one pair of scissors extra sharp. All she had to do was point to a picture in a magazine and Aunt Lil would try to cut it just that way. "Promise me," Aunt Lil would say, "one day you'll get away from here and get a real hairstyle."

Monsieur André held Mattie's chin and looked at her. "Blonder. To bring out your eyes. And we'll need to do something about the body."

He grabbed a handful of hair one more time, peered down at it, and called for his assistant to bring him the permanent wave lotion and the rods. Her hair needed more body—there was no doubt in his mind. He'd decided on Lana Turner.

She could have sworn after two hours of sitting in the chair and under the dryer that it was almost Lana Turner who looked back at her from the mirror. She hardly recognized herself.

"So much better." Monsieur André removed the pink wrapper, brushed her back and shoulders with a small whisk broom. He patted soft talcum powder on her neck. "Now you are ready to meet your fate." And he smiled at her in the mirror.

"Perfect," Flo said when Mattie walked through the door. "This calls for a celebration." She rang for the maid, a small neat woman with a head full of tight curls and skin the color of caramels. "Sheree, bring out the bottle of Cook's we've been saving and tell the girls to join us in the living room."

She slipped her arm around Mattie's waist. "It's like watching you go from a caterpillar to a butterfly overnight."

Charlotte put two fingers in her mouth and did a wolf whistle. "Don't you look swell." She hugged Mattie. "Next stop Hollywood."

Flo laughed and held up her glass. "To our newest star. To Mattie from Alabama."

Everyone raised their glasses and toasted Mattie and she stood in the middle of the room beaming until the doorbell chimed.

"Back to work," Flo said. "And don't forget to brush your teeth first."

"Mattie, honey," Evelyn said, "you're ready as you're ever going to be. Come on back to the office with me."

10.

THE pedigreed Pomeranian stayed unusually quiet in James E. Harris's lap. Lucius Augustus didn't like strangers. And Harris, slowly petting Lucius's long coat to conceal his displeasure, didn't like people coming to his house to talk business. He told Spence Voorhees before. But Voorhees was getting old. Harris could see it in the loose skin around his neck. His memory was slipping, his hearing was nearly shot. His eyes were going bad—he thought Lucius was a Pekingese. The meeting was starting badly; both James E. Harris and Lucius Augustus were in a snit.

"What was so important it couldn't wait?" Harris smoothed his midnight-blue brocade smoking jacket across his broad chest. Voorhees had caught him in the middle of his morning routine. Five newspapers, two glasses of orange juice—no pulp, no pits—two eggs once over lightly, thirty seconds at most. Toast with Robertson's orange marmalade, crusts removed.

"I have a strong curiosity about one of the new members of my District Committee," Voorhees said.

The houseboy brought in coffee in a silver pot, two bone china cups, a silver sugar and creamer on a silver tray. He poured a cup for Harris, then one for Voorhees. Lucius sat up and barked.

"Wait a minute, precious," the houseboy said to the dog. "Let Uncle Rex put some lumps of sugar in Daddy's coffee and I'll take you for a walk." With silver tongs, he carefully placed two lumps of sugar in Harris's coffee. "There now." Rex reached down to take Lucius in his arms. He kissed the dog's head. "We'll leave these big men alone so they can have their little chat." Rex carried the dog out of the room, his nose nestled into Lucius's neck.

Voorhees made a face.

Harris made a mental note of that face. Whatever Voorhees wanted just became harder to get. He waited.

"I'm not here to ask for help. What I'm suggesting is an even trade," Voorhees said.

Harris marveled once again that a man with so little tact and subtlety, with less intelligence than Lucius Augustus and half his tenacity, could have come so far in Congress. A man who had done nothing but lie blatantly since he graduated from high school. Harris knew Voorhees came from a poor family, not the one of distinction he claimed. His father was a hog farmer. Never did have a plantation. And Harris knew, as well, that Voorhees kept a small apartment on Capitol Hill where he entertained the several women he paid to be amused by him. One of the women, a Miss Vera Hudson, was also paid by Harris. But only for information.

Harris knew, too, about the money Voorhees received from the Klan during his last election. And which one of Voorhees's cousins still went to their rallies. He knew whenever Voorhees's wife slipped off the wagon. He knew about the trip to Switzerland for the monkey-gland operation. He knew which glass Voorhees put his teeth in at night. An even trade seemed unlikely.

"I'm listening," Harris said. With a man like Voorhees it never hurt to state the obvious.

Voorhees leaned forward, placed the fine china cup on the burnished cherry table. Harris noted Voorhees did not use the coaster. That table, along with the fine china and the silver, had belonged to his mother. "We've got ourselves a propitious set of circumstances, you and I."

Harris pulled out the small soapstone dog he kept in his pocket to soothe himself and relieve stress. Voorhees bored him and boredom was stressful. He ran his fingers over the cool, smooth surface.

"There's a bill coming up before my committee that would give you a choice piece of land for that building you've been wanting for your FBI. Of course, some people would rather see the land handed over to our War Department. One of the new boys might be willing to vote my way on this piece of land for you, if, and I say this with all due respect for how busy you are with more important matters, if I could learn a little bit more about him. I can usually read a man pretty good, but this boy's face is a blank slate."

"Let's be clear. What you're saying is you want me to investigate a member of your committee you think might be a threat to the safety of our country? Have I got that right?"

Voorhees nodded, spread his hands in front of him as if he were showing a winning poker hand. "That is precisely what I'm saying. This Andrew Stevens may intend to do harm to our nation. Then again, he may not. If you could put my mind to rest, I'd be grateful."

"What you're asking is almost impossible," Harris said.

He wasn't about to reveal that his natural inclination to distrust members of Congress forced him to keep extensive files on their backgrounds and activities. But this name—Andrew Stevens—was new to him. Not that it mattered. It wouldn't be hard to gather whatever information Voorhees needed— freshmen congressmen were rarely adept at covering their tracks.

The door opened and Lucius Augustus, freshly combed and dressed in a red plaid jacket, ran to Harris's feet. He leaned down to pick him up.

"Then I can take that to mean . . . " Voorhees said.

"Rex will show you out."

II.

MARCH 1941

1.

WHEN the clock slid past midnight and the regulars took their usual seats at the polished mahogany bar, Booker Wilson Jones let his hands run free and wild across the ivories. One by one other musicians would find their way to U Street, stagger into Tremaine's, pick up a drink, and join Booker on the bandstand. Late into the night, they dipped into their private reserve of songs so blue they turned the air the color of smoke.

Shorty Green, cornet to his lips, almost fell off the bandstand when he saw blond Daniel Granger, his brass buttons gleaming, his shoes high-shined, walk into the bar as if he were leading the Independence Day parade. Sergeant Callan was close behind. And six of his men behind him. The only white men in a part of town that didn't see many. And never this late at night. If any one of the people at the bar, at the small round tables, needed a policeman, they'd be hard-pressed to get one to come to this neighborhood. And yet, here were eight of them spit-polished and shining. Walking into Tremaine's like they owned the place.

Callan didn't want trouble. At least not tonight. This time his stoolie swore on his life Callan's vice squad would find whatever kind of vice they were looking for over at Tremaine's, after midnight. No double-dealing. He could tell from the looks on the faces of the men at the bar, they didn't know in advance he was planning to visit.

"Business or pleasure?" Tremaine said to Callan.

Callan couldn't keep a smile on his face if he wanted to. "Business."

Tremaine's wife, Delilah, in shimmering black satin with a white camellia in her hair, walked up to Daniel. "You don't look old enough to drink, sugar. Does your mama know you're out this late? Hanging out with this rough crowd?"

The people at the tables laughed the way they wouldn't have been allowed to laugh at any of the other bars in town.

"You got an office?" Callan said to Tremaine.

"Not unless you want to take out that toilet and put in a desk." Tremaine nodded to Booker Wilson Jones to keep on playing. He signaled to the men at the bar to keep drinking. He wiped his hands on a white dishtowel and came around to stand next to Callan. "Anything you want to discuss with me, you'll have to talk about right here."

"And anything you want to tell me about what's going on in that shack in the alley, you better tell me right now. Before we bust down the door."

Delilah took the camellia out of her hair and handed it to Daniel. "Here, sugar. You save that for when you take your sweetheart to the prom."

Daniel's face went red from forehead to chin.

Shorty Green picked up his horn and started playing "I'll Be Glad When You're Dead, You Rascal You," just like Louis Armstrong. The men at the bar, the couples at the tables, lowered their heads and laughed quietly.

"I don't want trouble," Callan said. "I just want answers. You got gambling back there?"

Wally Tremaine had broad shoulders and a neck so thick he couldn't find shirts to button closed around it. He had strong arms and powerful hands. He'd come up from the South and lived in Washington long enough to know he could get into as much trouble answering a question as he would ignoring it. Tremaine stood silent.

"I'm asking you a question." Callan pressed his nightstick against Tremaine's thick neck. "You got moonshine in there?"

"No," Tremaine said, sweat glistening at his temples. "I got supplies. I got toilet paper. I got a keg of beer and a barrel of rainwater. You find anyway for me to get running water and 'lectricity in that shack, you let me know. I've been thinking of expanding my establishment."

"Then you won't mind if we take a look." Callan had wedged his nightstick in the soft folds below Tremaine's chin. His head was tilted back, his throat exposed.

"Help yourself." Tremaine managed to reach into his pocket for his keys.

Callan released the nightstick, threw the keys in the air, and caught them with his good hand. "Why don't you show me?"

The men and women crowded around the small tables pulled their chairs out of the way as Callan and his men followed Tremaine past the bandstand and the restrooms into the narrow passageway leading to the backdoor and the alley.

The cold clear night carried the familiar alley smell of cooking collard greens and baking bread, overpowered by the odor of outhouses and garbage and families living five, six, seven to a room. Two skinny dogs lapped water from a pump in front of the shack next door. One dog caught the loose end of a clothesline and dragged it, clothes and all, across the cobblestones.

Callan almost stumbled over a rusted iron washtub. Tremaine handed him a flashlight.

"You are one cool customer," Callan said. He knocked on the door to the shack, slipped the key in the lock.

"Wait." Tremaine held his arm against the door to keep it from opening. "There is one thing I forgot to mention."

"Oh yeah." Callan pushed Tremaine's arm out of the way and pulled the door open.

"Brooms," Tremaine said. The flashlight lit up the storage shack. "Brooms and mops."

As they stared into the shack, filled floor to ceiling with rolls of rough toilet paper, a keg of beer, a barrel of water, three brooms and two mops, not one man in Callan's squad dared to even clear his throat.

2.

FRANK Henry Billings was so sure of his resemblance to Errol Flynn, he always carried a pen in his breast pocket in case he was asked for an autograph. He carefully brilliantined and waved his thick black hair the way Flynn did. His smile so much like Flynn's, they could have been twins. He should have gone to Hollywood, but he'd been too busy waiting for his ship to come in. And now, he thought, looking around the lavish apartment on Connecticut Avenue, it was finally at the dock. This new dame from Alabama might make a perfect figurehead. He needed to get a better look at her legs.

Flo hadn't told Mattie much about Frank. Only that he was the owner of the place she now called home. And he, of course, was her great benefactor, the one who paid for her new clothes, her blond curls, her three pairs of silk stockings. He was looking at her like he knew all that, he was looking at her like he owned her.

Flo said, "Just be yourself."

But he made Mattie feel not at all like herself.

Frank drank deep from his silver flask. Turned it upside down so she could see it was empty. "Must have a hole in it. We better get ourselves a bottle of Scotch if we're going to get to know each other." He rang the bell for Sheree. "A full one. Don't try to cheat me." He took out his cigarette case and offered her a cigarette.

"No, thank you, I don't smoke."

Frank grabbed the Scotch out of Sheree's hand, opened it, tipped it back, and drank. He waved the bottle at Mattie. "Now come sit on my lap and tell Papa everything else you don't do." He put his hand on her knee. "And all the things you do."

She could see the dark hair on Frank's knuckles and the dirt under his fingernails. His hand on her knee made her feel sick. Was she supposed to let him paw her? Why hadn't anyone told her what she was supposed to do?

"I'd better get us some glasses," Mattie said.

"A fancy one, huh? A regular Duchess of Windsor." Frank took his index finger and pushed the tip of his swollen nose in the air. "Think you're too classy for me?"

"Could you just excuse me a minute? I'll be right back." Mattie ducked into the kitchen. She stood by the sink and counted to ten.

Charlotte and Vera poked their heads into the kitchen from the other door. Charlotte checked her watch.

"You didn't even last five minutes. You'd think he was Joe Louis. Where's your courage? Where's your spunk? The guy's a cream puff."

"He's horrible. I just want to change out of all these clothes and throw them in his face. I feel like I need a hot shower."

"Shh," Vera said. She swung the door open halfway and peered into the living room. "Once he gets through a third of a bottle, he keeps his hands to himself." She let the door swing shut. "Looks like he's almost there."

"Come with me, please?" Mattie said. "I can't go back in there alone."

"Flo's not going to like it," Vera said.

"Oh, come on," Charlotte said, "it can't hurt if we keep her company."

"Not me," Vera said. "I did my time."

Charlotte grabbed three glasses and took Mattie by the arm. She swung the door wide and propped it open with her hip.

"Where's my Duchess?" Frank had slipped back so his head rested on the rolled arm of the sofa, his legs dangled to the floor. Scotch dribbled onto his white shirt. "Tell me the truth, girls," he tried to sit up. "Did you really think I was Errol Flynn when I walked in the door?"

"That's what Mattie said the minute she saw you," Charlotte said. "She said to me, 'You'll never guess who's here. It's Errol Flynn himself.' That's why she came to get me."

"I knew she looked like a smart one. C'mere. I won't bite." He turned his head and belched. "'Scuse me, I didn't mean to offend the Duchess." He slurred his words.

Frank gave Mattie a silly Charlie Chaplin kind of smile, then his face darkened. "Wait a minute, I get it. You think you're too good for me, don't you? One of those stuck-up Southern belles, aren't you? I know how to fix a tough little cookie like you."

He collapsed back onto the pillows. "What you need's a good spanking. That'll show you." He was asleep by the time he finished talking.

"There," Charlotte whispered. "All you have to do is wait for him to wear himself out. If only they were all that easy."

"Easy?" Mattie said.

3.

BETTY wore a red-and-white polka-dot dress, cut from the same pattern as her blue one. She tried something different with the front of her hair. She knew it was silly; the Congressman was eight years her junior. He probably wanted a family—a good-looking man needed a family to come home to after a hard day on the Hill. She was too old for children. But ever since her sister Joan saw that Jimmy Stewart movie where he ended up with his secretary, even though all along Jean Arthur thought he was a chump, Joan kept telling Betty she was sure Betty and the Congressman were headed straight down the aisle. Wasn't he always joking she was already like a wife? Stranger couplings had happened in this town.

Betty fixed her hair, fluffed it up a little, smiled at herself for being foolish, smoothed her dress over her wide hips, and fixed his breakfast tray. She added wheat germ to the orange juice. Since she'd been listening to Carleton Fredericks on the radio, she'd come to understand the power of wheat germ.

No sense nagging at the Congressman about sleeping in the office anymore—he seemed determined to live his whole life there. She'd picked up an extra shirt for him at Raleigh's Haberdasher and charged it to petty cash.

She placed a soft pink tulip from her garden on the tray. It might make what she had to tell him a little easier.

"Bad news, boss," Betty said.

Andrew groaned. It had been an awful week, made worse by the pain in his neck and back. He was starting to walk hunched over. It reminded him of Dirk Dykstra, the last congressman from his district. Andrew had met him at the Rotary Club dinner welcoming Dirk home from his six years in Washington. The man looked as if he'd returned from a war. His face was lined, what was left of his hair had gone gray. His double-breasted jacket couldn't hide his protruding belly. He still could smile and shake hands like a politician, but his shoulders were so hunched, he seemed to have grown shorter.

"Take a good look at your future," Dirk said to Andrew. "I was as young and eager as you are when I left." But then he pumped Andrew's hand and laughed his practiced laugh. "Just kidding. I don't think I was ever that young."

Andrew could have sworn he, too, was aging quickly. He looked in the mirror this morning and saw someone else looking back at him. A man with tired eyes and lines around his mouth. The shooting pain in his neck made it hard for him to hold his head up straight. His hand shook when he tried to part his hair.

"Okay, what's the bad news this time?"

"The Speaker wants to see you. In Room 103," Betty said. "Must have something to do with how you voted on that last transportation bill." She handed him the handwritten note requesting his presence at 7:00 p.m.

Everyone knew an invitation to Room 103 was a bad sign. They called it the Board of Education because it was reserved for congressmen who needed to be taught a thing or two about how Congress really operated. Only the black sheep got invited. Betty knew it was inevitable Andrew would be called there. She had hoped it wouldn't be so soon.

"If that old gasbag thinks he can bust my chops over whether I want a rat's nest of highways circling this city, he's wrong."

She nodded. She'd seen it all before—the young idealist who comes to Washington thinking he's going to change the world and he's the one who gets changed faster than you can say House Subcommittee on Appropriations for Agriculture and Forestry.

"It won't do you any good to go in there with a chip on your shoulder. So, I took the liberty of scheduling lunch with Congressman Winston. They're serving that bean soup you like."

She was always one step ahead of him. Maybe he should turn the job over to her and go back home instead of dragging out this misery. What had he been thinking when he agreed to run for office? "Thank you. Anything else?"

Betty sat down in the chair facing his desk. She took out her steno pad. She removed the pencil from behind her ear, careful not to mess her hair. "You've got those letters to the Michigan Mothers Against the Draft." She held her pencil ready for dictation.

"Let's get to that later." The pain made it hard to think.

"Whatever you say, boss. But don't blame me if they show up on your doorstep one day. Not the kind of attention from women a man like you is used to." Betty stood and smiled in a way that was almost flirtatious. She tried not to go overboard, but once Joan put the bug in her ear, it was hard to get it out.

Funny, he thought, she looked more youthful, just as he was starting to look like an old man. She seemed to sway her hips a little more than usual. She turned coyly—or was it his imagination? —and said, "Oh, one more thing. I got a call from the girl in Congressman Voorhees's office. He's arranged an appointment for you over at the Franklin Institute. She said he discussed this with you already. She said it was important enough to make sure I clear your calendar for tomorrow afternoon."

"Fine," he said, but he couldn't remember talking to Voorhees about a Franklin Institute. Well, whatever it was, he knew he better go along. He was in enough hot water already.

Betty started to turn one last time to smile at the Congressman, then her good sense kicked in. Back at her desk, she pinned her hair down flat, the way she always wore it. No fool worse than an old fool. And there were already too many of them around Capitol Hill.

4.

MATTIE and Charlotte sat next to each other on red stools at the counter in Schwartz's Drug Store, both drank thick chocolate malts. Like everything else, it was Flo's idea. She thought Charlotte could help Mattie get over her nervousness. The phones were ringing off the hook. But twice Mattie claimed to be sick and stayed in her room all day.

"If you tell me what's bothering you, I promise I won't laugh." Charlotte held up her hand, three fingers in the air. "Scout's honor."

Mattie shook her head. She kept drinking her malt, though she bit down so hard on the paper straw, half of it came off in her mouth. She fished the shredded pieces off her tongue with her fingers.

"I lied," Charlotte said, as she watched Mattie struggling. "I am going to laugh."

Mattie blushed.

"Look, kid, whatever it is, I've probably heard worse."

"It's just that you all, what you do," Mattie said, her cheeks still flushed, "I'm not . . . I mean I'm still . . .what I'm saying is I've never."

Only the truth was, maybe she had. She still wasn't sure about whatever it was she and Charlie Baker had done in the back of his Chevy Standard. They'd fumbled and groped, all zippers and buttons, feverish mouths and hands. Afterward, she was achy and sticky; awkward and afraid to look at him. Afraid to see him again because she might be tempted to finish what they started. Unless, of course, they'd done that already. But you couldn't tell someone as sophisticated as Charlotte you didn't even know if you were still a virgin.

"I think I know what you're trying to say." Charlotte rubbed Mattie's arm. "We don't expect you to do anything you don't want to do."

Mattie studied Charlotte's green eyes to see if she were lying or joking. "You don't?"

"Not unless you want to. Besides," Charlotte lowered her voice, "that's not what we do. Not there anyways."

"You don't?" Mattie still wasn't sure if Charlotte was lying.

Charlotte called for the check. She slid off the red stool and nodded hello to one of the men at a table in the back. He pulled down the brim of his gray fedora to let her know he'd seen her. Charlotte wouldn't say another word until they were on the sidewalk.

"Kid, it's all kind of complicated. We've got to stay just this side of the law if we want to earn enough to keep body and soul together. It's already illegal to give a member of the opposite sex a massage."

"Now, I know you're joking. Illegal?"

"Here in Washington. But we've got influential friends in this town who are willing to look the other way. Especially the ones who enjoy a nice steam bath now and then. Anything more than that? Well, you won't see that happening at Flo's place."

"Wait," Mattie said. She tried to head Charlotte in the direction of one of the benches that ringed Dupont Circle. "If you're going to keep pulling my leg like that, we better find some place to sit down."

"I'm not saying that's all that goes on when someone goes to a party at a hotel room or a private home. Flo's got a dozen women around town she can call on for those requests. But at the Institute, all you're expected to do right now is just give a massage and keep them happy. Maybe go for a dinner or two."

"But what if they want . . .?"

"You roll your eyes and say, 'Maybe next time, sugar,' in that sweet Southern voice of yours. Geez, half the men in this town got where they are by promising something they never intended to deliver."

Mattie hated to disappoint everyone who'd been so good to her. But she was scared. She wasn't as naïve as they thought. Smyrna wasn't so far from Nashville that she hadn't heard stories. *Fallen women*, her momma called them, *pure white trash.* They ended up unwed mothers, shunned by everyone. Or they took drugs, drank whiskey, and walked the streets until someone came along and beat them up. She remembered a magazine story about a woman strangled by one of her customers with her own stockings. That wasn't how she wanted to end her days in Washington.

"Aren't you ever afraid of getting hurt?"

Charlotte shook her head. "I'm not saying it can't happen. But Flo runs a pretty exclusive place. No one gets in without a recommendation or an interview. Funny thing is, you'll have a hard time finding a better job. I don't yet know of one place that will pay a woman even half of what she's worth and treat her as well as we get treated."

They'd walked all the way up Connecticut Avenue to their elegant apartment building. The magnolia tree to the right of the entrance with its large white blossoms and shiny green leaves almost hid the Franklin Institute plaque. For all anyone knew, it could have been a place for scientific research. Mattie felt as if her life from now on would be one big experiment.

"It's too late to back out now. Besides," Charlotte turned to look directly into Mattie's wide hazel eyes. "Don't try to tell me you're not just a little bit curious."

5.

TOM Callan was sick at heart. He threw the newspaper on his desk. A front-page photograph showed the Baltimore police raiding a brothel. "Baltimore." He shook his head in disgust. How could the police in that seedy, two-bit, piss-pot of a town strike it rich while his own squad kept coming up empty?

He smelled a rat. His informant was nothing but a double-dealing, no-good bum. Someone else must have been paying him more to keep the cops chasing their own tails. He stayed awake all night devising a new plan. He'd use that new boy Daniel Granger. But he didn't trust him alone—the kid was too green. He'd pair him up with Arnold Burns.

"I've got a special assignment," Callan said to his men. "And I'm looking for volunteers." He paced the room and looked at them. In the early morning light, they all looked pale and weak, pitiful. Only Daniel met his eye, everyone else looked at the floor.

"There's a place in Georgetown I've had my eye on." He stopped and glared at them. They knew better than to laugh whenever he made reference to his eye. The men were silent. "I'm sending two of you in there."

For the first time since he joined the force, Daniel didn't look at Sergeant Callan. He hung his head and kicked his heels against the rung of the chair.

"You're not going to accept the full range of services. You know as well as I do that's against the law, but I need you to find out what they're offering." What he was asking them to do was risky. The last time he sent in two cops to check out a place from the inside, they succumbed to temptation. He hated like hell to kick them off the force, but he had no choice.

"Burns," he said.

Arnold Burns sat up straight. "Yes, sir." He barely met the height requirements. He'd been lucky on the weight. But lately his uniform fit a little snug. He'd have to get back in shape before the next physical. He couldn't afford to lose this job. His wife was pregnant again while the first one was hardly a year old. He sucked in his gut. "Ready, Sarge."

Callan drummed his fingers on his desk. He looked around again and the men squirmed. "And . . . " He paused so long he could feel the tension in the air, "Granger."

Daniel jerked his head up. "Me, Sarge?" The other men shook their heads. The kid just couldn't learn to keep his trap shut.

"You. You could use the experience."

"Yes, sir," Daniel said in a voice so miserable it was hard not to hear a note of fear.

Callan walked to the spittoon and spat. "There's nothing to be afraid of."

"I know, Sarge, but I'm a Catholic, and I . . ."

Callan slowly withdrew his nightstick and slammed it on his desk. "I don't care if you're the Pope himself, as long as you've got a clean shirt and a good pair of pants."

Daniel nodded.

"Here's the address and phone number." Callan handed the paper to Burns. "You call and make an appointment. Say you're new in town. You let them take it from there."

6.

THE waiter in the dining room at the Occidental couldn't have been more attentive if they'd been royalty. The two women, impeccably dressed and terribly sophisticated, requested a corner table. They each wore hats with dark mesh veils concealing their faces. Movie stars, perhaps? They both had that incandescence. It wasn't often he saw women dressed this well—the ones who came into his restaurant were as dowdy as the First Lady herself. Women in Washington seemed to take pride in being unfashionable, which was why it was such a pleasure to wait on these two. Women who ordered martinis at lunch instead of the usual sherry.

Flo Maxwell glanced once around the dining room to make sure she didn't recognize anyone who could recognize her. Serena Diego did the same, sweeping the large brim of her black hat across the table, nearly toppling the salt and pepper shakers.

"The news it is terrible," Serena said in her heavy Spanish accent. She lifted the dark veil to sip her martini. She never removed her black calfskin gloves. She wore one strand of white pearls around her neck. A matching strand around her wrist.

Flo, her gloves removed, her square-cut emerald ring exposed, gracefully wrapped her hand around the glass, her red lacquered nails catching the light.

"No one's hurt or in jail?" Flo said.

"Not yet. But the times are getting very bad for the women of our businesses."

The waiter refilled their water glasses, asked if they'd like another cocktail. Would they care for caviar first or perhaps steak tartare?

"Two soles of the filet," Serena said to the waiter who seemed unable to leave them alone. "Now be a good boy and let us to ourselves. We have much business to discuss."

Three men, prominent lawyers from the large law firm down the street, passed by their table. Serena nodded slightly at the first one. She lowered her voice. "We must be careful not to say so much."

"But you've said nothing," Flo said.

They were not rivals and yet they often competed for the same clientele. Though Serena, with her fear of police, with her constant dramatic worries she might be deported, kept her business open only during the day. Only during the week. She kept the hours of the bankers, she liked to say. She served tea and cookies. Upon occasion, for foreign diplomats—especially the French—she would serve coffee.

Her tidy Georgetown row house with the white ruffled curtains could have been home to someone's grandmother. It could even have been, as the sign said outside, the home to The Horticultural Association.

Serena could call the business anything she wanted. She owned it. But Flo could do nothing. Frank owned the Franklin Institute. That was the name he picked and that was the one they'd keep. He liked the official ring and the not-so-subtle link to bawdy Ben Franklin.

"I have heard from a friend," Serena said, "there are people in this city who wish to put the wool in our eyes."

"Put wool in our eyes?"

"Yes. They wish to make fun with us. To play tricks with us."

"What kind of tricks?" Flo never knew when Serena was telling the truth or being melodramatic.

"It is like what we hear about in Germany. The police, they will come right into your house. They will take away your business. They will take away your freedom. These police, they come in costumes."

"Costumes?" Police in costumes? Was this more of Serena's penchant for cloak and dagger?

"Maybe it is not costumes. But what you call the simple clothes."

"Plainclothes?"

Serena nodded. "That's it. They are under the covers." With one black-gloved hand she took a roll from the silver bread tray. "The police they are coming in their plain clothes to fool us. They are coming to arrest us. They have received orders to do this. They will put us all in jail and I will be sent back to my country without a trial."

"Where did you hear this?" Flo thought she had reliable sources, but no one had told her about this. She thought she had an understanding with the police. Spencer Voorhees practically guaranteed they'd be left alone.

Serena smiled. "You know I cannot tell this to you. But I trust the person who has told me. He is one of the large ones, very important. He tells me it is not only the police in Washington who wish to arrest us. But also, those government police you hear on the radio."

"The FBI?" That seemed so unlikely. They usually went for criminals who could grab headlines—gangsters and communists. They wouldn't be wasting their time on small business operators like the two of them. "I don't believe it."

Serena shrugged. "I tell you this because you are my friend. You must be careful now. They will be watching us."

Their fish half-eaten, the roll basket empty, Serena motioned for the waiter to bring their check.

Flo rose to kiss Serena goodbye. Then she spotted Congressman Voorhees and another man threading their way past the table. She sat down again.

"One more thing," Serena said. "They are also arresting the boys with the bells."

Wasn't she laying it on a little thick?

"You know. The ones in the hotels who take the suitcases and call us for the parties."

"Bellboys?"

"Yes, exactly. The men from the churches want to punish those boys for helping us. That is all I can tell you. Now we must go."

Serena bent down, her hat brim knocking against the brim of Flo's hat, knocking their veils askew as they kissed each other on both cheeks. "I will let you know if I see any police. You will do the same for me?"

"Of course, I will," Flo said. "But everyone is so worried about the war, I'm sure they've got more important things to do."

7.

CLINT spread the photographs on Harris's desk. "This one's not bad."

Harris put on a pair of white cotton gloves. He held the photograph to the light. A glossy of Spencer Voorhees sitting in an arm chair in the apartment he kept on Capitol Hill. A redhead on his lap. Harris hated redheads. "Doesn't surprise me."

"And this one." Clint handed him a photo of Voorhees and the red head standing—Voorhees was unzipping her dress. "Too bad he couldn't follow them up the stairs. That's the best he could get."

"It's enough. Down there in the Bible Belt they don't need more than this to turn a man out of office. And wouldn't you say from the looks of this picture it's pretty clear this girl is a mulatto? They always dye their hair red."

The only ones who didn't were the ones who thought they could pass, like those two women who ran that place on Connecticut Avenue. Florence Maxwell and Evelyn Gardner. As if those were their real names. As if anyone could get anything past him.

"We've also got a recording. Sounds like Voorhees has a talent for animal sounds."

"Must be the result of that monkey-gland operation."

"Should we send the photos?"

"Not yet. Let's hold on to these for a while, Put them in the private files."

Clint unlocked the door to the adjoining room filled with file cabinets floor to ceiling on three walls. The first cabinet's drawers were filled with photographs of men who were used to seeing their pictures on the front page, making news as captains of industry, political leaders. These photos told a different story. Hundreds of photos of men and women, half-dressed, undressed, a few of them dressed in each other's clothes. The next wall of file cabinets held recordings and transcripts, most of them made Voorhees at his most obscene sound like a choir boy. Another wall of cabinets held the reports. The fourth was the trophy wall covered with grainy and glossy, black and white framed photographs. Each one of a well-known criminal stretched out on a slab, wearing a white sheet and a toe tag.

Those were their best days. Every time they caught a bank robber or kidnapper, Harris insisted on getting a final portrait—one copy for the newspapers, one copy for his private gallery. The photos of Voorhees, with his skinny white legs and thick garters holding up his thin black socks, could never elicit the same thrill.

Clint bent to open the bottom drawer of the photo files, but the drawer was so heavy it sagged to the floor. He got down on one knee to keep the drawer from slipping off its track. He wedged the new folder in carefully. The glassine envelope with the negatives would go into the vault in their bedroom.

When he stood, he could see a hint of dust on his trousers. He brushed furiously at his knee, slapping away the smallest trace of dirt. There'd be no time to change; they were leaving in five minutes. Harris had a speaking engagement at the District Social Hygiene Society.

8.

FROM the front porch, Daniel heard his mother and her two brothers arguing in the kitchen. He hoped he could sneak into the house, grab his good clothes, and be back at the station before his mother knew he'd been there.

"Just because he's happy, Kate," Quinn said, "doesn't mean the boy is simple."

"He's too good-natured to be a cop. Don't know how he let the two of you talk him into it," Kathleen Granger said. "He'll never have the heart to arrest anyone. And Lord spare us what he'll do if they give him a weapon. He'd be better off with a desk job or working in a bank."

"At least you didn't decide he should be a priest," Liam said.

The screen door squeaked. There'd be no sneaking into the house today.

Daniel found his mother and two uncles sitting at the Formica kitchen table. They each held a cup of his mother's homemade brew. That meant trouble. She only passed it around when she felt poorly. Otherwise she sold it all to the few Irish taverns still operating private bottle clubs after the other bars closed.

"There he is, the boy himself," Quinn said.

"The word is you're making quite a name for yourself on the force," Liam said. "We've heard that one-eyed bandit Callan has taken a shine to you."

"Ask me," Kathleen said, and it never mattered that no one did. "I still say it's unnatural. The boy should be studying. He should be finding himself a wife. Instead, he's working day and night."

"Day and night, is it?" Liam winked at Daniel. "I'll sleep safer, knowing that."

"Treating you well, are they?" Quinn said.

"Definitely," Daniel said, not sure how much he should mention about his new assignment. Not sure how much he wanted his mother to know. "I've been put on special duty."

"There, you see," Liam said to his sister. "He's on his way to sergeant already."

"And what exactly is this special duty?" Kathleen said.

In spite of himself, Daniel blushed. "I'm . . . uh . . . I'm . . . um, not at liberty to say."

"I'd bet you two bits it's nothing less than our national security the boy is protecting," Liam said.

"I wouldn't be surprised if the President himself gives him a medal," Quinn said.

"And I wouldn't bet I've heard one honest word from the whole lot of you," Kathleen said.

9.

THE minute Daniel Granger and Arnold Burns walked through the door, Serena Diego knew they were the police in costumes she'd been warned about. She wore an ugly brown-and-white house dress she had bought in case her worst fears turned out to be true.

"Can I help you?" Serena said.

Arnold made Daniel promise to let him do the talking. "We've got an appointment," Arnold said. He tried to wink, his chubby cheeks bunching up under his eyes.

"You are with the *For Ay Chez*?" Serena said.

"The four what?"

"*Ay Chez.*"

Arnold shook his head. Daniel tapped him on the shoulder. "Now what?"

"I think she means the 4-H Club," Daniel said.

"Yes." Serena smiled at him.

Arnold started to sweat. He was staining the one good white shirt he owned and his wife would kill him. He couldn't tell her why he needed to wear it. He said he had to go to a funeral.

"No," Arnold said. "We're not from the 4-H Club. We've got an appointment." He put a lot of emphasis on the word appointment. But Serena looked at him blankly.

"You know." He cocked his head toward the stairway.

"Wait. I think I understand what it is you want." Serena called up the stairs to someone named Cecile. "Could you come down, my dear, I think these gentlemen are here for seeing you."

Arnold smiled at Daniel. "What did I tell you? Leave everything to me."

Arnold looked around the room. It could have been his grandmother's living room. He expected to see a honky-tonk piano player and girls in skimpy clothes with black-mesh stockings and red garters on their thighs. He expected to be fawned over by a handful of beautiful women. Instead he saw an old tea service, a plate of cookies. A fireplace decorated with pine cones and wreaths. Small china figurines on the mantel.

Cecile, in a blue house dress even shabbier than Serena's, came down the stairs. Her hair was set in tight pin curls held in place by dozens of bobby pins. She wore bedroom slippers, heavy tortoise-shell eyeglasses. She carried a ball of wool, two knitting needles.

"Please forgive me. I forgot your appointment. Maybe I can help you anyway. Let me see." She picked up one of the brochures lying on the table in the front hall. "You were interested in growing orchids? I think this explains everything you need to know. We have meetings at the end of the month. You're a little early."

"There must be some mistake. We're not gardeners. We're just a couple of Joes who got the name of this place from one of our buddies. Didn't we?" He elbowed Daniel.

"That's right. We're new in town and looking to . . . um . . . hmm." He cleared his throat. "We're looking to have a good time."

Cecile looked at Serena; they both shrugged. "I'm sure our members enjoy themselves when they get together. But there are no meetings today. Maybe you'd like a cup of tea?"

Arnold shook his head. "Something's fishy here. Would you ladies mind if we look around?"

"Look around?" Serena said. "We would very much have the mind. In fact, if you don't leave right now, we will call for the police. You do not have the rights to barge your way like this."

Out on the sidewalk, looking back at the lace curtains, at the sign that read Horticultural Association in big brass letters, Arnold tried to collect his thoughts. It was three strikes in a row for Sergeant Callan. Arnold didn't want to be the one to tell him. He wouldn't take it well.

"Okay. Here's what we do. When we get back to the station, you tell the Sarge someone must have given him the wrong address. He likes you, so he won't get so mad. You don't tell him anything about what went on in there. You don't tell him how we made fools of ourselves talking to a couple of ugly old maids who thought we were interested in growing orchids. No man in his right mind would mistake those old biddies for the kind of broads we're after."

Arnold started to throw the brochures in the trash can near the curb but Daniel stopped him.

"If you don't mind. I'd like to take these home to my mother. Maybe make her stop worrying so much."

10.

ANDREW was sick of meetings. First, he'd had lunch with John Winston. Even his one good friend in town felt obliged to remind him of all the things he didn't know.

"You don't know how things operate. You don't know which of these boys you can trust." John gestured to include all the other members of Congress who were eating in the restaurant. "And you don't know how to get what you want."

Andrew nodded. Everything John said was painfully obvious.

"But that's not the problem. The real problem is you're too impatient. Too headstrong and too damn stubborn. You're a friend, so I feel like I owe it to you to tell you."

"Hate to hear what you'd say if you didn't like me so much."

"I know you're frustrated. Hell, everyone here is frustrated. There's always someone who's gonna be standing in your way. The trick is learning how to get around him before he pushes you aside."

Over bean soup and grilled veal cutlets, he watched as John, senior representative from the Great Lakes state of Michigan, and one-time star quarterback for the Wolverines, lined up the silverware and napkins, the salt-and-pepper shakers, and the bottle of Worcestershire sauce to show him how to block and tackle, pass and punt his way off the District Committee and move higher up the ladder.

All John's advice hadn't done him a bit of good in his meeting last night with the Honorable Horace P. Hoffman, Speaker of the House, and resident scold. The Board of Education meetings were Hoffman's way of keeping maverick congressmen in line.

"You know why you're here," Hoffman said.

Andrew shook his head. Hoffman was the first person who gave him credit for knowing anything.

"Maybe this will help." Hoffman slid a folder across his empty, polished desk.

Andrew opened the file marked with his name in red letters on a plastic tab. And there it was—his whole life. Only maybe not the way he would have told it if he'd been asked. On the first page, it listed his suspicious activities. His questionable associations. With labor unions. With his college roommate Gerald, who was Jewish. With his old girlfriend Lorraine, whose best friend was Negro. With Lorraine's ties to the orphanage. His meetings with the auto workers. His support from the machinists. His interest in the Youth Congress. And the article he wrote for *Law Review*. They knew everything right down to his shoe size and the last time he bought a package of Trojans.

"Frankly," Andrew said. "I'm baffled by all this."

"Well that makes two of us. I'm baffled by how you could have taken an oath to serve this country when it seems clear to me your sympathies lie elsewhere. Let's hope they don't see fit to call you before the committee investigating un-American activities. Be a sorry day for all of us if they do."

Fifteen minutes of that and he was on the phone with John as soon as he was back in his office.

"You never warned me about this. I feel like someone's been poking around my life."

"Someone has. Sounds like Spence Voorhees is up to his old tricks. Now tell me exactly what you said to set him off."

Andrew swore he didn't have a clue.

"When's the next time you're going to see him?"

"I don't know," he said. "No, wait a minute. Betty mentioned something about Voorhees making an appointment for me tomorrow at a place called the Franklin Institute. The way I'm feeling now, I'd better cancel."

"Absolutely not. If he's taking you to the Institute, it must mean he's not ready to throw you to the wolves just yet. I can't give you any strategy for how to handle this one."

Was it possible he heard John laughing?

"You've got a reputation for being someone who can think on his feet. Hope that's not the only way you can do your thinking."

How could he have gotten himself into so much hot water so fast? All he'd done since he arrived in Washington was work in his office. He led a quiet life. And yet here he was, next in line for his picture on a poster of the FBI's ten most wanted criminals.

III.

APRIL 1941

1.

VOORHEES left a message for Andrew to meet him at the Institute. 2:00 p.m. sharp.

Andrew assumed it was a group of scientists conducting research on weapons the country might need for war. He didn't want to keep them waiting. Strange to find it in a residential neighborhood.

He recognized a few of his colleagues on their way out of the building. He spotted one of his favorite baseball players coming through the door with a man he thought was the owner of the team.

Andrew straightened his tie, smoothed his jacket. Betty was right. He was grateful to have the new shirt she bought him.

"There you are," Voorhees said when a short buxom woman escorted Andrew into the sitting room. Voorhees held a drink in one hand, the arm of a small blond woman in a nurse's uniform in the other hand. "I was afraid you were shying away from me. Glad to see you're made of stronger stuff, boy."

"*Vee-rah,*" Voorhees drawled, "you got someone special you can assign to my young colleague here? This boy's got pains running up and down his neck like a wild fire in a field of dry oats. Surely, you know someone who can help him."

"Got just what the doctor ordered. Make yourself at home," Vera said to Andrew.

"Grab yourself a bourbon and soda. And while you're at it, freshen up this one for me." Voorhees held out his glass. "Don't look so frightened, boy. You are about to get one of the finest *may-sah-ges* you can get in this town. If this doesn't get you standing up straight again, nothing will. The way I hear it, you are carrying the weight of the world on your shoulders these days."

"Certainly feels that way."

Andrew looked around, slowly getting a sense of the place. He tried to absorb the whole awful impact of where his bad luck had landed him this time. He took in the fancy furnishings, the marble floors, the velvet sofa and chairs, the crystal chandeliers, the gilt-edged mirrors, all tastefully done. And yet, even though he'd never been to one before, he was sure this so-called massage parlor was actually a brothel. High-class and elegant, but a brothel. He was certain the women, all dressed in white uniforms like nurses, all reputed to be certified masseuses, were each willing to provide what was referred to as "other health-giving benefits."

"I told you I had the solution to all your problems," Voorhees said.

Andrew was speechless. He checked his watch. "Unfortunately," he said, not meeting Voorhees's eyes, "I've got another meeting scheduled. I can't stay. I'm sorry." He turned to leave.

Just when he was sure there could not be any more impossible surprises waiting for him; just when he was convinced not one thing in this crazy town could ever go right, Vera came back into the room with a striking young woman. His loneliness, so thick it could have been another person, whispered what he felt was love at first sight.

"Mr. Stevens," Vera said, "this is Alabama's pride and joy. I'd like you to meet Miss Mattie."

2.

"COME right this way, Mr. Stevens." Mattie tried not to sound as nervous as she felt. Everyone was watching her. No one had to tell her if she didn't do well with her first client, she might soon be without a job, without a home. As she walked ahead of Andrew, the sound of her heels clicking on the marble floor filled the enormous silence.

Voorhees said Andrew should think of this as one of the perquisites of the job. Sounded like more Southern snake oil to cover what was clearly an illegal operation, benefiting from the patronage of the one man in Congress who could shut it down.

Mattie opened the door to room number five. She smiled as brightly as she could. "Just step this way."

Andrew entered the room. Mattie hesitated at the door. Was it his imagination or did she seem as nervous as he was?

"I'll give you a few minutes to remove your clothes and slip into this." She didn't look at him when she handed him the white terry cloth bathrobe. "Make yourself comfortable on the table, and I'll be back to give you a Swedish massage."

He could hear the lilt of a Southern accent. He could see her hands were shaking. "It's just my neck. My shoulders and my neck. I'm not interested in anything else. So, I'm sure I don't need to . . ." He held out the robe to give it back to her. "Don't you agree?"

Mattie could see Flo watching her from down the hall. She stepped closer to Andrew, guided him back into the room. She shut the door behind her. "I'm sorry." She was almost pressed against him. "This is my first . . ." She twisted the bathrobe's belt in her hands. "I might lose my job if I don't do this right. You really need to change into the robe so I can do the massage properly."

Andrew's chin almost rested on her head—she was that close to him. There wasn't enough room for him to take a step back so he could look at her. He was afraid she might be crying.

"All that's bothering me is my neck. If you can get rid of this pain that's been driving me crazy, I'll tell them you did everything right." He wanted to touch her face, to brush the hair away from her eyes.

Mattie took a deep breath. "Thank you."

She'd been afraid to look at him before, but now she could see he had a handsome face, kind eyes. He was the best-looking man she'd seen since she came to Washington. Grown up in a way Charlie never could have been. Not that it mattered. He was a client. And she'd been told by everyone at least a dozen times she was never, ever to get involved with a client.

"You're from Alabama?" He said and immediately knew he must have sounded like an idiot. He probably wasn't supposed to talk to her.

"Really, it's Tennessee," she said, and the conversation ended right there. Was she supposed to talk to him? That seemed to make it more awkward for both of them. If only she could call in Charlotte.

Mattie helped him remove his jacket. She loosened his tie the way Charlotte showed her. She unbuttoned his shirt, helped him slip it off. She motioned for Andrew to lie on his stomach on the long white table. When her hands stopped shaking, she put a dab of scented massage oil in her palm, breathed on it to warm it, pressed her fingers into the base of his neck.

He lay on the table. Too many thoughts raced through his mind at once, then stopped when the strangest sensation came over him. It was like the moment on a late summer morning, the minute after the crickets ceased their constant racket. He gradually realized, after all these agonizing weeks, the pain that hadn't let him out of its grip was gone.

3.

AFTER he left, Mattie's fingers still tingled. She was surprised at how much she liked the curve of his neck, the fine blond hair that trailed down his spine, the warmth of his skin. He'd been kinder than she expected. Not at all what she thought congressmen would be like. She thought they'd be old and stuffy. Jowly and paunchy, like Spencer Voorhees. Instead he was young and handsome. If only they'd met somewhere else— at a dance, at a party. If they'd bumped into each other at some place as ordinary as the A&P.

"Mattie." Charlotte knocked softly on the door. She opened it a crack. "Flo wants to see you in her office as soon as you're ready."

"Did I do something wrong?"

"From the way you're smiling, I'd bet you did everything right. It's probably just routine."

Flo had a thick red ledger book on her desk next to a small vase filled with flowers, alongside another vase filled with pencils. A photograph of Marian Anderson in front of the Lincoln Memorial hung on the wall behind her chair.

"Don't look so frightened. He left here a happy man."

From what Voorhees told Flo, they could count on Andrew as a regular. Voorhees would know. He'd brought them half a dozen of his colleagues. He was always generous in sending visiting businessmen their way.

Flo caught Mattie blushing. "Think you're going to stay a while after all?"

"I'm not planning on going anywhere."

"That's all I wanted to hear. Now there's one or two things we need to get straight."

Mattie looked around the room again, sure this was the time when they'd bring in the Devil himself so she could sign her pact with him. Where else was all this going?

But Flo only wanted to show her the large red leather ledger book where she kept track of the business. It was easy to follow how Flo kept their accounts.

"Like everybody else, we've got expenses," Flo said. "First, there's Doc."

Mattie had seen the little bald man with the large black bag racing around the apartment last week. Charlotte told her he wasn't as bad as he looked. He had a weakness for Hershey bars and funny ideas about prescribing vinegar and lemon douches. You could talk him out of giving you medicine if you kept a few chocolate bars on hand for him.

"We pay Doc a monthly retainer. And then there's Frank."

Mattie looked at Flo, then looked away. She hoped she'd never have to see him again.

"You're not the only one," Flo said. "But right now, he owns this business. We hope someday, if we can put together enough money, we can buy it from him. This book," Flo held up a small black notebook the size of her hand, "is like our savings account passbook. If we gave Frank all the money we made, he'd drink it away and there'd be nothing left for us. As it is, he only pays me fifty dollars a week. What he wants me to pay the rest of you is chump change. So, we each put something away in here that Frank doesn't know about. It's our insurance policy. We keep track of clients and sometimes we add a few names of important men, even if they've never visited the Institute. That way if we get raided . . ."

"Raided?" Mattie's uneasiness returned. She shouldn't be doing this. She should have gotten a job at the Red Cross.

"Hasn't happened yet, and if we're careful, it never will. But we need to protect ourselves. We've got a lot of friends, but we've also got a lot of enemies." Flo watched Mattie's smile fade. Maybe she really wasn't cut out for this life.

"I'm sorry I mentioned it. You've got nothing to worry about."

"Good. Then I better get back to work." Mattie got up to leave.

"Just one more thing." Flo opened the small black leather book. She picked up a pen. "I need you to tell me exactly what Congressman Stevens likes."

$$4.$$

BETTY hesitated before knocking on Andrew's door. He had kept it closed ever since he returned from that meeting at the Franklin Institute. It wasn't like him to close his door. And he had such a strange look on his face.

She opened the door a few inches, poked her head in the office. "Are you all right, boss?"

Andrew stared out the tiny slit of a window behind his desk. His swivel chair was broken. He'd have to get up out of his seat if he wanted to face Betty. And he didn't want to face her, not yet. He was smiling. That would get him in trouble as fast as anything he'd done so far. No congressman ever smiled if he wasn't campaigning.

But when he thought about Mattie, he couldn't help himself. She was remarkably pretty. Young and fresh and, strange as it seemed given the circumstances, there was something so innocent about her. She had such a lovely profile, it could have been etched in ivory on a cameo. He was struck by it the first time he had seen her nearly perfectly heart-shaped face. If only they'd met somewhere else. At a reception, at a cocktail party. If only she'd been one of those visiting nieces his colleagues' wives were so eager for him to meet.

He tried again to make his chair swivel, gave up, and stood. He cupped his chin in his hand before he turned around. "I'm fine."

"We ought to get your chair fixed," Betty said.

"What?" He was remembering the funny way Mattie walked when she was nervous.

"The chair. Get it fixed. So you won't keep straining your neck."

Andrew rubbed his neck. "My neck is much better, actually."

"Ah, that's what it is. Must be a great relief."

"What?" He touched his neck where she had worked her magic. Her fingers were surprisingly strong for someone who seemed so slight. Slight but tall. His chin almost rested on the top of her head when she stood close to him. She was maybe five-foot-six or seven. She smelled of lavender, gardenias, and lilacs all at once.

"You're a million miles away. I've got a good mind to leave you there. Anything you need me to do before I go?"

He was still rubbing his neck, still standing there with that silly expression on his face. "No. Wait a sec. Yes. Could you get Voorhees's secretary on the phone and ask . . . No, wait. Maybe I ought to do it myself. I don't want you involved."

"Sure. Whatever you say." Betty backed out of the doorway.

Who was he kidding telling her not to get involved? When her own life was already so intertwined with his she'd never get it untangled? Not get involved? What town was he living in?

5.

"AND isn't the boy seeming strange to you lately?" Kathleen asked her brother Quinn.

"Not that I've noticed. He's a grown man now, Kate. You can't keep watch on him the way you did when he was a child."

"Someone's got to. If I leave it up to him, with his innocent nature, he'll get taken advantage of by the first sweet-talking girl who comes along."

"And when is the day you'll let him talk to a girl?"

"That's where you're in for a surprise. I've invited Brigid Ryan to supper tonight."

"How is that letting him have his own life?" Quinn had been like a father to his nephew Daniel. And like a father, he'd been trying for years to help Daniel cut the long ties to Kathleen's apron strings. But every time Daniel pulled away, Kathleen pulled back harder.

"A girl, is it?" Liam said. "We've got names for people who provide those services. What will you be bringing him next, I wonder?" Liam was the family tease, with a twice-broken nose to prove it. He had always been more like Daniel's older brother.

"I'm done with the lot of you," Kathleen said.

Daniel hoped to sneak in through the back door this time. His face still burned from the chewing out he and Arnold had just received from Sergeant Callan.

"Still here?" Daniel said, when he opened the door to find his mother and uncles gathered again at the kitchen table.

"A shirt and tie?" Quinn said. "Doesn't sound like the old Tom Callan to me. What did you say you were doing these days?"

Daniel's face couldn't get any redder. He stooped to tie his shoelace, answered his uncle with his mouth so close to the floor, the words barely made it back up to the table.

"Never mind all that," Kathleen said. "You need to freshen up. There's a shirt of your father's I've saved all these years. You're old enough now, you might as well have it. We've got company coming."

"Then you'll be wanting us to stay," Liam said.

Quinn started to set the table.

"I was hoping I'd get to bed early," Daniel said.

"Working that hard, are you?" Quinn said.

"Nonsense," Kathleen said. "With all that work, you'll never find yourself a wife. Brigid Ryan will be here any minute. Now go, get ready."

He hadn't seen Brigid in years. When he went to Gonzaga, she went to the Academy of the Holy Cross. She chose secretarial school and a government job over life in a convent but, as his mother often reminded him, Brigid still went to Mass every morning.

"A lovely girl," Kathleen always said. "Sweet as they come."

The shirt was too big. Daniel's father was a large man, who'd grown larger in memory in the twelve years since he'd died. Daniel couldn't fill his shirt, fill his shoes, couldn't stop his mother's constant worrying, couldn't finish school, and now, he couldn't please Sergeant Callan. That's how his mind was working when he came back downstairs.

With the cuffs of his father's shirt hanging down over his hands, his face washed, and his hair freshly combed, Daniel answered the door on the first knock.

And there was Brigid, in a plaid skirt and white shirt, looking like the stocky and sturdy schoolgirl he used to know.

She smiled shyly but hugged him in a way that left no doubt it had already been agreed between Brigid and his mother she was the girl he'd been waiting for.

6.

LIKE it or not, Mattie was learning the business. Evelyn kept her booked every day. Only the easy ones, Evelyn promised her. Until she was ready to move on. In the meantime, if anyone got demanding, if anyone got rough, she could call on Sam to show him the door. And whether or not she wanted to admit it to herself, she didn't mind the work. For the first time in her life, she felt independent. If her momma could see her now. But Charlotte kept reminding her the best part was her momma never would.

Mattie put on her new white uniform. White high-heeled shoes with open toes. White stockings. Evelyn told her this afternoon one of their best customers, a Mr. Allen Mears, owner of the largest car dealership in Philadelphia, was bringing in his son as a present for his birthday. It didn't get any easier than that. She checked her lipstick, fixed her hair. When Sam rang her from the front desk, she was ready.

She was expecting a young man, just out of adolescence, but even before he turned around, she recognized him. She remembered the light blond hair on the back of his neck, and the broad shoulders she'd thought about once or twice.

"Mr. Stevens? I didn't expect to see you so soon. How's your neck?" She hadn't seen his name on the schedule and she knew she was booked for the whole afternoon.

Andrew didn't have the nerve to call Voorhees's office to get the phone number. Instead he took a cab over on an impulse, a crazy whim, something he'd never done before, but he had to see her again.

"You must be some kind of miracle worker. My neck is fine."

"I didn't see your name on the schedule today." She liked his smile all over again and the sparkle in his blue eyes.

"I was hoping we could talk. Get a cup of coffee."

Flo and Evelyn made the rules very clear. If a man wanted to take you out, for a drink, for dinner, even a cup of coffee, he needed to make an appointment through Sam. No private socializing. No last-minute dates. Business was business. And pleasure? Making money should be pleasure enough. They were not allowed to fraternize with their clients.

"I wish I could." She knew Sam was watching her from behind his desk. Flo said they'd all be keeping an eye on her for her own safety. "If you'd like to see me, you can make an appointment."

"I don't understand. You don't seem like the type of girl . . ."

Don't let them get possessive, Charlotte warned her. If they do, they make your life a living hell. And here stood Andrew Stevens, after meeting her once, looking at her the way Frank had, as if he owned her.

"You mean the type of girl who'll drop everything the minute a man wants to see her?"

Why was everyone twisting his words? "That's not what I meant. I was hoping . . ."

He saw how she looked at him. It wasn't the way he imagined it last night when he stayed awake thinking of her. "All I wanted was coffee. Look," he took out his money clip, held out a ten-dollar bill. "I'll pay you for your time, if that's what you want." He didn't know why he kept talking. He could tell he wasn't making the right impression. Still he went on, took out another bill. "Not enough? Tell me how much?"

Sam got up. No one was allowed to pay any of the women directly at the Institute. When the drunken businessmen came in and flashed their cash, when the baseball players showed up on pay day and threw their twenty-dollar bills in the air, they were always escorted out.

"Is he giving you any trouble?" Sam said.

"Thanks. I can handle this myself. You'd better put your money away," Mattie said to Andrew. She looked straight into his angry blue eyes. "I am the type of girl who's not for sale." She turned and walked away.

7.

"WHAT kind of sucker do you gals take me for?" Frank Billings asked Flo and Evelyn. "You think I don't know what's going on here?"

"Keep your voice down," Flo said. "You're upsetting the girls."

"Upsetting the girls? You don't think I'm upset? Get me a drink. And don't go calling that fancy little yellow maid you have here either. Unless you want me to be the one to tell her she's out of a job."

Evelyn didn't bother to look at him.

"Frank," Flo said. "Listen to me. You can't just waltz in here like this and start causing trouble."

"Why can't I? I own the whole damn place." He grabbed Flo by the arm, rubbed the sleeve of her silk blouse between his fingers. "I own you and everything you've got. So don't tell me what I can and can't do."

"Relax." Evelyn set down a new bottle of Scotch, clean glasses. She plumped the pillows on the sofa. "Sit back. I'm sure we can work this out."

Frank had arrived unannounced with a young woman he had met in New Jersey. He drove her down so he could give her a job at the Franklin Institute. She had a figure that could stop a clock. What else could they want? Lucy Dee, short for Deevine, would be their next star.

"She's too young," Flo said. "You know we can't let her work here."

"Turn around for them," he said. And Lucy turned slowly in front of Flo and Evelyn. "The rest of you broads got backsides like brewery horses. Not one of you can hold a candle to her." He pinched her fanny. "Can they, doll?"

Lucy smiled serenely. Men had been pinching her fanny since she was twelve. Nineteen felt more than old enough to finally get paid well for it.

Frank found the divine Lucy working at Minsky's Burlesque House in Newark, New Jersey, as a fan dancer and striptease *artiste*. He stuffed enough dollar bills in the glorious valley between her breasts to get her to agree to drive to Washington with him. He promised to replace the old rabbit fur wrap she used in her act with real ermine. He said he'd set her up for life. It was his business, wasn't it?

"We don't have room," Evelyn said.

"Make some," Frank told her. "You can kick out that new little number who thinks she's too good for the rest of us. No headlights anyway. Or else maybe that old hag Charlotte, who's looking a little used up."

"Definitely not," Flo said. "No one is leaving."

"Then you better start sleeping on a cot, since this doll baby is staying." He pulled Lucy onto his lap. He tickled her ear. "I'm counting to ten. When I'm done, I want to hear from both of you this fine young woman has a position in this establishment. Otherwise, you'll be the ones out of a job."

"It's too risky," Flo said.

"Didn't any of you ever hear of the good old American practice of lying? Women lie about their age all the time."

Evelyn shook her head. "Frank, you're not being practical. If we take her on, we're the ones who end up in jail. If we agree, you've got to promise you'll let us handle it our own way. No more interference from you. No more surprise visits. You stay out of this and leave it all to us. Agreed?"

Evelyn watched him guzzling the booze. She and Flo had decided ahead of time when he got to the point where he turned soft and sloppy, Evelyn would try to strike a deal to keep him out of their hair for good. He was bad for business, worse for morale. The girls got nervous and depressed whenever he came to town.

Frank, his head tipped back, snored in fits and starts. Evelyn tapped him on the shoulder. "Agreed?" He opened his eyes long enough to say, "Yeah, sure." His head fell back and the snoring began again.

Flo took Lucy by the hand. "Lucy, honey, why don't I show you around. You'll see, it's almost like a sorority house here."

8.

"LOOKS like someone's got a secret admirer." Charlotte carried the bunch of violets into Mattie's room. Billy, the delivery boy from Rock Creek Florists, trailed behind her. The girls treated him like a kid brother. They never had to give him a tip if they let him wander around the Institute for a few minutes. Ever since Lucy arrived, Billy was finding excuses to stop by every day. He liked to bring her lemon drops.

"Are they really for me?" Mattie said.

"Says so right here on the card," Charlotte said.

Mattie stood for a minute holding the flowers, holding the card, shaking her head. Billy was off peeking around the corners, trying to catch sight of Lucy coming out of the shower.

"Don't you want to find out who they're from?" Charlotte said.

Mattie opened the small white envelope. *Hope this is the right way to apologize to a girl of your type,* it said. She held the violets closer to inhale the sweet scent, to hide her pleasure.

"Bet that smells just like trouble. Kid, you better come with me. There are still a few things we have to teach you."

Mattie listened over lunch while Charlotte and Vera, Flo and Evelyn told her stories about the dangers of taking up with a client. *It's for your own good,* each one said. Sheree chimed in as she served them cold salmon with fresh mayonnaise. Mattie was asking for trouble, they all agreed.

"If I had a dollar for every man who wanted to rescue me," Charlotte said, "I'd be rich enough to buy this place and everyone in it."

"All guys get some crazy idea they can save us," Vera said. "But talk about out of the frying pan."

Lucy was late to join them. "At least get some good jewelry out of it." She opened a small velvet pouch, shook four rings onto the table. "This blue one was from Count something-or-other." She placed it on her left index finger. "Awful, awful man. He never cut his toenails. And this one," she slipped a small ruby ring on her right pinky, "was from the man who invented the radio. I swear on my life that's what he said. These other two were what you call 'brief engagements.'"

"One day I'll show you the love letters," Evelyn said. "Stacks of them."

"Trust me," Flo said to Mattie, "he may be the first but he won't be the last. We just don't want you getting hurt."

Sam interrupted them to say Congressman Voorhees called to make an appointment for Congressman Stevens. Flo said to schedule him with Lucy.

"But . . ." Mattie said.

"We'll go to the movies," Charlotte said. "When's the last time you saw a good movie?"

"Can't I just say thank you? Where I grew up it's not right to ignore someone if they give you a gift."

"Mattie, honey," Flo said.

That was all she needed to say for Mattie to understand she would not be allowed to see Congressman Stevens. Not allowed to take his phone calls. Not allowed to be at the Institute when he arrived.

Charlotte made them sit through the *Maltese Falcon* twice. It brought back her yen for cigarettes and she'd sworn off Luckies two weeks ago. She bought three bags of popcorn. They were still eating from the last bag, still talking about what they'd do if Humphrey Bogart ever showed up on their doorstop, when they nearly ran right into Andrew as he was coming out of their building.

"Look who's here," Charlotte said, checking her watch.

"You planned it?"

"Guess I'm just a soft touch," Charlotte said, with a wink.

"Where have you been? I did what you said—I made an appointment—but you weren't there," Andrew said.

"I'm sorry." Mattie tried not to look at him. She tried not to like him. "I can't see you again."

"You can't or you won't?"

The doorman held the door open as they stood halfway inside. People going in and out stepped around them. Andrew took Mattie's arm to lead her out of the way. She jumped when he touched her.

The doorman opened the door one more time and Voorhees, his face flushed from the steam bath, his thin hair still wet, came barreling through the door.

"I can see you're doing a little private lobbying," he said to Andrew. "Hope you'll be back in time for our committee meeting. I was counting on your vote today."

"We were just saying goodbye," Mattie said.

"Good." Voorhees wrapped his arm around Andrew's shoulder. "Ride back with me. I've got my driver right here." Without so much as a nod to Mattie, Voorhees walked Andrew to the car.

Before he got into the backseat, Andrew turned once to look for Mattie, but she'd slipped inside the building.

9.

"HAVE you completely lost your mind?" John asked Andrew before he closed the door, leaving Betty straining to hear the rest of the conversation. A glass to the door, her ear to the glass, she could barely make out what they were saying.

"Do you know how long it took to get around the cloakroom you not only climbed in bed with some call girl but succumbed to Spence Voorhees's charms as well?"

"I'll never get used to this being such a small town."

"I can see that."

The next exchange was garbled. Betty couldn't tell for a minute who was talking. Something must have been said about Andrew's career. She heard John, say, "Lonely? We can fix that." More mumbling. Were they laughing? And then a phone call to Senator Doyle's office.

Everyone knew Senator Doyle had the most eligible daughter in town. Pictures of her at horse shows, small as a professional jockey, always walking off with a medal, filled the Sunday magazines.

Photos of Emily Doyle in elegant ball gowns, on the arm of some diplomat's son, decorated the morning newspapers. Betty had been reading about her for years. Emily Doyle was the closest thing to a celebrity in Washington.

Betty's nose tickled. She felt a sneeze coming on. She had to step away for a minute. The feeling passed and she was back in time to hear the name Emily Doyle again. "Perfect for each other," John said. "Everyone's blessings." Andrew good-naturedly said she'd probably never hold a candle to Hattie? Addie? Mattie? It was a name Betty hadn't heard before. Lowered voices. Andrew said, "No, we never. She's not what you think."

That tickle was back and Betty missed everything except "home to mother." And then they sounded angry again. John said, "Do you want this job or not?" And Andrew answered quietly, "I'm no longer sure." Their voices dropped so low she lost all of it. Was John telling Andrew to grow up? Andrew said something, something, "just this once," and "nothing to lose." John, his voice deeper and louder. "Good. I'll stop by to pick you up at seven." She was back at her desk before he opened the door.

She was at the same desk early the next morning. News about his evening also arrived before Andrew walked through the door. She knew he'd left the reception with Emily Doyle.

They were seen having dinner at the Hotel Washington. Betty's source—the little red-haired gal in the Senator's office—claimed they'd been seen holding hands. News enough to make the social pages in the morning newspaper. A small item about one of the most eligible bachelors in town seen kicking up his heels with a well-known senator's lovely debutante daughter. Was this the start of a new political dynasty?

Andrew, earlier than usual, was showered, shaved, and whistling a tune. She'd never heard him whistle before.

"Sounds like a nice evening," Betty said.

"It was, actually. How did you know?"

She slid the newspaper across her desk.

"Well, well," he said, shaking his head, but smiling. "News does travel fast around here." He walked into his office and closed the door.

A few minutes later the phone rang. When Betty answered, the young woman, breathless and giggling, was already talking. "Emily Doyle for Congressman Stevens. My Andy's not some big old lazybones still asleep at home, is he?"

Betty was a sucker for romance. Take her to a movie with Clark Gable or Gene Tierney and you'd better have an extra handkerchief along, she'd most likely bawl her eyes out. She wanted only the best for her boss—a more decent young man had never set foot on Capitol Hill. So, she didn't need to take the trolley to F Street on her lunch hour and spend all her money on Madame Canova, the astrologer and clairvoyant, to suspect the Congressman's new romance looked a little shaky.

10.

A broken clothes line, rotting porch steps, weeds in the small square of land that passed for a backyard. When he wasn't working, Daniel's weekends were filled with chores and errands for his mother. Kathleen's list was endless.

"Never mind all that," Kathleen said as Daniel tried to fit a patch of mesh onto the small hole in the screen door Kathleen found on her last inspection. "Isn't it a fine day to take Brigid to Glen Echo Amusement Park?"

Daniel was speechless. Kathleen always said work and church were amusement enough. But now, she told him, a bit of fresh air, a few wholesome rides were far better than the two of them sitting alone in the dark watching a movie. Who knows what they'd get up to?

For once, Daniel had to agree with his mother.
He hadn't been to Glen Echo in years—his uncles had taken him for his twelfth birthday. They teased him for weeks about how he gasped when the trolley suddenly turned away from the river and veered off into the woods. Daniel loved the Big Dip coaster and the bumper cars. His first and only time in a swimming pool, they couldn't coax him out.

"In my time it was very romantic," Kathleen said. "That's where your father proposed."

Romantic? Propose? When he wasn't even sure if he liked the girl. He and Brigid seemed to be plodding along.

Doing what was expected—Saturday night dinners with his mother, Sunday suppers with her family after church. He wasn't enjoying it much. Maybe his mother was right. Maybe a trip to the country would be a good change.

But the sweet shyness Kathleen admired in Brigid was what made it so hard for Daniel to take her anywhere. She wasn't against having fun, she just didn't see the point. She was determined to lead a pious life. She hoped to find a husband to share her dream of joining a missionary service in Africa. Kathleen let it slip she'd always believed her son would be more suited to the missionary way of life. All he needed was someone to guide him in the right direction.

Brigid agreed to go to Glen Echo only if her little sister Peg could join them. Why else would they want to do something so silly?

And there was Peg sitting next to Brigid for the trolley ride out. The two of them whispering and giggling, ignoring him. They didn't even look out the window.

When the trolley stopped at the entrance to the park, a group of teenagers scrambled out ahead of them.

The guard approached the three teenage boys who were last in line. "Hold it right there," the guard said. And the boys stopped laughing and talking.

The shortest, in a clean white shirt and khaki-colored pants, emptied his pockets to show he had a handful of quarters to spend, just like everyone else.

"You can put that money away—admission is free. Except to you boys," the guard said. "This is whites only. Always has been, always will be. If you boys could read, you would have known that. Now how would it look if we let you three swim in that nice Crystal Pool?"

"Daniel, can't you do something?" Brigid said. "You're a police officer."

Daniel already had his badge out. He told the teenagers to wait, he was sure he could help.

"You can put that badge away, won't do any good here," the guard said. "This is private property. Why don't you take your family inside and let those boys take care of themselves?"

"But they're with me. They're part of my family," Daniel said. "No reason we can't all go in together."

"If that's how you want to be, then you can just turn around and get right back on the trolley. All of you." The guard blocked their way.

Peg stamped her foot. "Why'd you have to ruin it?" she said to Daniel. "You're as bad as she is." She pointed to Brigid and stuck out her tongue. "I hate you both. I hate having to be your chaperone. You never have any fun."

Brigid took Peg by the hand.

"No," Peg said. "I don't want to go home. You're fat and mean and you'll never get married."

"Would you really tarnish your soul for some cotton candy and a roller coaster?" Brigid said to Peg, but she looked at Daniel.

The trolley conductor rang the bell one last time and the three of them traipsed back on. Brigid wouldn't say another word until Daniel walked her to her door. She pecked his cheek and said she'd see him at church Sunday morning.

The day had been a disaster. Daniel couldn't sleep. He spent the night wondering how to tell his mother he might not be cut out for marriage after all.

"Well, the fresh air didn't do you a bit of good," Kathleen said at breakfast. "I don't know how you'll get that sweet girl to marry you if go around looking like something the cat dragged in."

IV.

JULY 1941

1.

FOR the first time since she left home five months ago—was it that long?—Mattie wasn't sleeping well. She lay awake and heard the clock ticking, the apartment settling. She heard again her mother's voice on the telephone. It sounded wavery and watery and not at all believable when her momma assured Mattie there was nothing wrong—she just needed a small operation. There wasn't any hurry; the doctor said it could wait until she had the money to pay for it. Then Aunt Lil got on and whispered to Mattie what she already feared. It was serious. Her momma needed to go to the hospital as soon as possible. Was there any way she could send more money? Aunt Lil hated to burden her but with her good job at the Red Cross, maybe they'd see their way clear to helping someone in need? Otherwise, Aunt Lil started to say, but Mattie said there was no reason to worry about otherwise—she'd send the money.

She sent home a few dollars every week. As much as she could afford. Once Flo got her share and Frank got his, once she paid what she owed for her room and board, there wasn't much left. The last time Frank visited he waved a twenty-dollar bill in front of her face, pleading with her to give him one night alone. He passed out before he heard her refuse him.

She rolled over, shook her head to get the image of Frank out of her mind. It was going to be a long night.

When she was a child, her momma would give her a cup of hot milk with a tablespoon of honey and a pat of sweet butter to help her sleep. She'd almost forgotten but now that's all she wanted. She was sure they had a jar of honey in the kitchen.

She tiptoed out to the hall where she put on her robe and slippers, still not paid for. How would she ever find the money for her momma with all these other debts she'd run up? Flo already told her there was a policy on not giving advances. Once they started doing that, their whole operation would fall apart.

A light was on in the kitchen. Mattie could see the shadow of someone at the small round table. The shadow of a milk bottle, twice its real size, against the wall.

"Am I glad to see you," Lucy whispered. "Pull up a chair and join me. Hate to celebrate alone." Lucy still wore her evening gown. One beige satin strap, studded with rhinestones, had slipped off her shoulder. She'd taken off her shoes, draped her stockings over them. She wore her pink garter, decorated with one white flower, on her wrist. Her lipstick had rubbed off her lips and her mouth looked pale, but her cheeks, her chin, were red. Her eye make-up made two dark streaks down her face. She propped up her head with her hand and smiled a drunken smile. "What an evening. Had the best time of my life."

Mattie wasn't sure how it happened, but Lucy moved right in as if she'd always lived there. No one had to handle her with kid gloves. No one had to show her the ropes. She was the one who was a natural. Even thought she was the youngest, she seemed more like an old hand. Within a week, she was as busy as the rest of them, while Mattie still struggled through the easy ones.

"Can you keep a secret?" Lucy blinked her eyes to stay awake. "Look what I got." She reached down into the bodice of her dress and pulled out three fifty dollar bills. "Just for one night. Beats my own record. Never knew magazine publishers were so filthy rich."

Mattie didn't know what the other girls made—the ones who performed the "extra services." She never asked and they never told her. She knew Vera could afford better clothes and Charlotte could always be counted on to pay for a soda or maybe a taxi. All her momma needed was three hundred dollars.

"Is that the usual amount for, um . . ." Mattie said.

"Stop the music," Lucy said. "You mean you don't?"

Mattie shook her head.

"Not ever?"

"Never." Mattie was beginning to realize all that fumbling with Charlie hadn't been as serious as it seemed when it happened.

Lucy laughed so hard she almost knocked over the milk bottle. "And you live here? I'll be a monkey's uncle. Bet Frank doesn't know, does he?"

"No, and he doesn't need to." She'd forgotten Lucy was Frank's latest pet.

"Don't worry about me. I don't mind keeping him in the dark. Probably where he crawled out from in the first place." Her own joke got her laughing again. Then she stopped. "You're scared, aren't you? Because I swear on my mother's head there's nothing to worry about."

"Not for you, maybe."

Somehow Lucy sobered up a little. "Oh, sweetie, you just do what the Reverend Norman Vincent Peale says, concentrate on the positive and you can do anything."

Lucy sat up straight, slipped the satin strap back up on her shoulder. "Isn't a woman alive who couldn't do it with her eyes closed. There's just three rules you gotta' remember. First off, no kissing on the mouth. You save all your tenderness for someone you care about. Which is the second rule. You don't let yourself care about any of them. Never fall in love. You keep your heart locked away, nice and private. And the third rule is you keep yourself clean. That's not such a big problem here. Flo runs a very high-class operation. But you can't be too careful. You wait three minutes, and then you get yourself into the bathroom, get washed, dressed, and get on home. I hope I don't have to tell you to get paid ahead of time 'cause once they roll over and go to sleep, there's no getting anything out of them."

Mattie nodded, added another teaspoon of honey to her hot milk, nodded again.

"Hey," Lucy tousled Mattie's hair, "it's not so bad. A person can stand anything but hanging is what I always heard. Even at your age, you still look like a heartbreaker. We just gotta' teach you to have a tough skin. The rest is as easy as falling off a log."

"Nothing to it," Mattie said.

"Wait a sec," Lucy said. "I've got an idea that'll solve everything. You busy tonight?"

2.

ANDREW'S father had been mayor of Muskegon, president of the Rotary Club, and a lifelong member of the Elks. He played golf at the country club, poker at the Big Bear Saloon. He did it all, he said, so his son would have a shot at getting elected to the US Congress.

But Vincent Stevens had not worked so hard so his son, his blond-haired blue-eyed boy, could turn out to be a liberal. And a Democrat, with a capital D. A friend to those unions that made his own life hell.

If his father had been around to say it, he would have been the first to say it was a good thing he died before he saw his son get elected to Congress with the backing of Chicago money and the union boys.

Andrew thought it would be a relief to come to Washington where no one recognized his name. No one knew his father and no one knew the very public and painful rift between them. He thought it would be a blessing that freshman congressmen were expected to keep quiet their first year or two on the job. But he'd been wrong on all counts. He couldn't trust his own judgment any more.

He'd been ready to hand his heart to that pretty young girl he had met at the Institute. And look what happened? No, he was going to take John's advice. Stick to the party line. Find a nice girl everyone would approve of. Get established. Then change the world. He could certainly do worse than Emily Doyle.

She came from a good family with good connections. She was bright and perky and if she'd just stop talking baby talk in that high breathy voice, they'd be fine. More than once he caught himself responding in baby talk. Each time, he hated himself for it.

She'd practically been hand-chosen for him and she didn't seem to mind. On their first date, she asked him if he'd consider living in New Hampshire once his term in Congress ended. She grew up in Washington but wanted to raise her children in New England. They'd need a house with land enough for their horses.

And now Emily was calling to invite him to dinner with her parents at the Chevy Chase Club on Saturday night. Surely he had formal attire?

He could picture her cooing and smiling while she said, "If you don't, we can get Daddy's tailor to make you a tuxedo." Senator Doyle, a man he'd met once, had already become Daddy.

"Thanks," he said. "I can manage."

"Good. Don't worry about not having a car. Daddy will send his driver for you. "

Andrew started to fidget. The pain in his neck returned. He could feel a headache working its way behind his eyes up to the top of his head. "Why don't I get us a cab and we'll meet your parents at the Club?" Though he wasn't sure where he'd find the money for the tux, the taxi, the dinner. And he'd be expected to bring her flowers.

"You are a silly one this morning, aren't you? You have to promise me you won't be difficult. Daddy told me you might be. He said you were getting a reputation for being naughty. And I told him nonsense—my Andy is gentle and sweet as a lamb. Aren't you?"

Andrew still kept his bottle of aspirin on his desk. He took two and answered Emily at the same time. It came out sounding like, "Nrrnghh."

"I knew you'd say yes. See you on Saturday. Toodle-ooo."

Toodle-ooo? He took another drink of water and called for Betty.

3.

THE cards weren't falling Callan's way; he was ready to play a different hand. Chief Coker called him on the carpet for telling his men to make appointments at the cat houses. No more, the Chief thundered at him.

Everyone knew the Chief's piles were acting up, making him meaner than usual. From now on, the Chief told him, he was only allowed to follow up on complaints from the johns who'd gotten rolled. The Chief wanted him to cool his heels waiting for the complaints, cooperating with the Feds whenever possible.

Cool his heels? Callan wasn't going to give up on raiding one of those bawdy houses. He would just go at it from another angle. He wanted those women off the street for good, not going through some revolving door at the jail every time they got arrested. Those women deserved to spend the rest of their days behind bars. It was not a personal vendetta.

He'd completely forgotten the one time he tried to pay for the services of a woman and she'd been so sickened by the sight of him, she forced him to take back his money and leave her alone. He put it out of his mind the night it happened and never thought of it again. He'd been young and foolish and easily tempted. He wanted that temptation gone for good.

But there was no end to the kind of vermin living in Washington. The newspapers were riding the police hard to make the District of Columbia safer now that it was on view for all the world to see. Heads of state were coming in every day from Europe, from the Far East. If they didn't find a city pure as driven snow—it was Callan's ass on the line.

And what Chief Coker wanted, he said, wincing with pain every time he sat down on the rubber donut on his chair, was for Callan and his men to zero in on the queers who seemed to think Washington was their own private picnic grounds. Worse than the hookers, they'd come to prey on the servicemen. And they were turning up everywhere, Coker told him. In public restrooms. In boarding houses. In theaters and night clubs.

An easy enough assignment. It didn't take much to spot them and it didn't take long to catch them. Callan's men were rounding them up and piling them into police wagons nightly.

It was all going smoothly until the night Daniel Granger came to see him. He held his cap in his hands. He twisted it so hard, he almost broke the hat band. "We've got a kind of situation, Sarge."

"What kind of situation are we talking about?"

"We were responding to a call about something funny going on in the restroom at the National Theatre. It turns out we arrested a couple of gentlemen who think they were picked up mistakenly. I swear, Sarge, we caught them, um, red-handed."

"Where are they now?"

"Outside in the car, sir. They said they're not coming in. They said we should call Congressman Voorhees and he'd take care of everything."

"Voorhees is one of those prissy boys? He does have that look, doesn't he?"

"I'm not sure what you mean, sir."

"Never mind. You get any names? Any kind of identification?"

"One of them is in Congress. The other works for the FBI. I swear, Sarge, we didn't make a mistake. We got this off one of them." He showed Callan a riding crop.

Callan almost smiled. He finally had some evidence.

"You did just fine." Without thinking, he reached out his twisted hand and patted Daniel on the back.

4.

IT was only a cocktail party and then dinner at the Hotel Washington. On the roof if the weather held. He was a Southern gentleman, polite, genteel, and dripping in money thick as Spanish moss, Flo said. And now that Mattie had taken the plunge, she might as well get one of the plum assignments.

Mattie thought she'd feel cheap but once she saw how much money men were willing to spend on her, she discovered she felt very expensive.

When she looked at herself in the mirror, in the simple black cocktail dress, the single strand of pearls, her curls even blonder, she was sure her momma would see the signs of sin all over her face.

It was all Lucy's doing. Or maybe undoing. A double date with two Italian diplomats, gentle as lambs, Lucy promised. A bottle of expensive champagne. A bubble bath in a luxurious hotel. Sheets as smooth as silk. He was kind and patient, as Lucy promised. And Lucy was there to giggle with her when she sneaked back into her own room at two in the morning.

"Aren't Italians wonderful?" Lucy said. "The older the better—they're less demanding. More grateful. They fall asleep faster. Next time we'll try French."

Mattie promised herself she'd quit as soon as she had enough money for her momma's operation. Maybe go back home and take care of her momma. She wasn't sure she liked herself any more. She didn't like the little shiver of excitement she felt getting dressed up, going out to dinner on the arm of a distinguished gentleman. If he was old enough to be her father, it didn't bother her. She'd never known her father.

Her escort for the cocktail party was silver-haired and honey-tongued. He put his hand on the small of her back and glided her through the crowd as smoothly as if they'd been a pair of ice skaters. He was lobbying the House District Committee to let him build a new hotel downtown. Mattie knew he needed to stop and talk to everyone who was there eating the shrimp and drinking the champagne he'd paid for. He kept her glass filled, kept his arm around her waist—she missed it every time he took it away to shake someone's hand.

That dreadful Spencer Voorhees almost drooled down the front of her dress when he stopped to say hello to them. He gave them both an evil wink.

Her escort was so tall and regal, towering above all those short congressmen, she almost felt proud to be on his arm. He eased them over to someone his own height.

"You must be Congressman Stevens," he said, tapping Andrew's shoulder. "I'm Jimmy Dupree. The hopeful builder of a new hotel in your beautiful city and your host for the evening."

Andrew turned to shake his hand, but in the crush of people around them, he touched Mattie's hand instead. They both acted as if they'd received an electric shock.

"Easy now. I know she's a knockout, but I'd hate to see you land on the floor. Miss Mattie Simon, this is Congressman Andrew Stevens."

Mattie nodded, smiled shyly, sipped her third glass of champagne too quickly.

A small blond woman in a sea-green chiffon dress pushed her way through the crowd toward them. "Andy candy, you gave me a scare. I didn't know where you'd run off to." She stood on her toes to kiss Andrew on the side of his neck. Her dress cut so low, her breasts seemed to swell and float out of the sea-green foam.

Mattie tried hard not to smile but the champagne was making her giddy. "I'm sorry. Did you say Andy Candy? That's kind of sweet." She tucked her arm in Jimmy Dupree's.

"I was hoping you'd join us for dinner," Jimmy said. "You and your wife."

Andrew started to correct him, but Emily squeezed his hand.

"You and I have never had a chance to talk," Jimmy said. "I think it would do us both some good. "

"I'm sorry, we've got other—" Andrew said, his eyes still on Mattie.

Emily held her hand up for Jimmy to kiss and said in an altogether different voice, one with a deeper, sexier tone, "We'd be charmed."

"I think," Jimmy said, one hand on Mattie's waist, the other one around Emily's, his eyes drawn to all that sea-green foam, "the pleasure is mine. We should have ourselves quite an evening."

5.

LUCY'S tricks worked surprisingly well. All Mattie had to do was let her mind take her somewhere else and she could almost forget the man on top of her. Sometimes it shamed her to think Charlotte might have been right all along, this came too naturally. She imagined what her life would be like when she had saved enough money to move out on her own. She'd get her own place and a different job. She'd be free to meet the kind of man she wanted to marry. She could picture him tall and slim, with blond hair and blue eyes, and the nicest smile.

As Mattie lay on her back on the queen-sized bed in the Hotel Washington, with the distinguished Southern gentlemen trying to move things along slowly but rushing in spite of himself, when she tried to picture the man of her dreams, Andrew appeared instead. She shook her head to clear it.

"Did I hurt you?" he whispered.

"Not at all," Mattie said, her voice soft and low. "You're doing fine." She hoped she hadn't set him off his rhythm.

"Not too fast for you, am I?"

Lucy said, "Just tell them they're fine. Even wonderful, if you can make it sound sincere. And when you get really good, you say they're the best. That's all they want to hear."

Mattie closed her eyes and there was Andrew again. This time she lay still. No use fighting the inevitable. She relaxed and let Andrew fill her thoughts.

That was all it took for the distinguished Southern gentleman. "Thank you, thank you, thank you," he whispered.

Mattie was dressed and out of his room before he opened his eyes to look for her. Smiling at the elevator operator, walking past the desk clerk's knowing stare, nodding at the house detective, she held her head high, kept her back straight. She checked her watch—less than a half-hour. And she had fifty dollars more to send to her momma.

6.

CALLAN'S sources seemed to be more reliable. He went out on a limb on the last tip—a Shriner's convention at the Shoreham Hotel. He heard they hired women. He also heard they hired men. People thought they could come in from out of town for a night or two and do whatever they wanted. It was like catching fish in a barrel. His squad ranked first in the department for arrests in the past two months. Just let Coker try to keep him from becoming lieutenant now.

But Coker, so red in the face he looked as if he might have a stroke, wanted more. Congressman Voorhees was leaning on Coker. There was some under-the-table deal between Voorhees and Harris for a new FBI building. Talk of turning policing the District over to Harris as well. Coker wouldn't give in without a fight. Neither would Callan.

Callan was up all night, tossing and turning. His wife said she hadn't gotten a minute's rest herself.

"What's eating you?" she said at breakfast.

They were a clean-cut family. Church goers. The wife knew he dealt with the lowest of the low. But he never told her more than that. He'd wait and let her read about it in the newspaper when he became the city's next hero and got his promotion.

"Just the usual." He read the paper. Ate his oatmeal. Kissed her goodbye on her forehead. Her lips had become so paper thin and dry.

At work, he thumbed through the newspaper again. He skimmed the funny pages; they weren't very funny these days. He browsed through the classifieds. Soon he and Margaret would be able to buy a house in Maryland. One with a lawn. He glanced at the rest of the ads and then something caught his eye. It was what he'd been looking for. He left the paper lying open on his desk and called in Granger and Burns.

"I've got orders from the Chief we have to be a little more careful in how we go after these hookers. If we make an arrest before we have the goods on them, the charges won't stick and they'll be back on the streets before you have a chance to fill out the paperwork. As it is, they're getting off with only a fine. No one's locking them up. No one's making them get treated for VD. It's enough to make you sick." He walked to the spittoon, spat in it, wiped his mouth with the back of his twisted hand.

"So, we've got to take our time. Set up an airtight case. I'm going to have some of the boys stake out a few of the places. But what I want you two to do is get yourselves jobs as desk clerks at the Marco Polo Hotel. From what I hear, they've got twenty, thirty couples checking into the same room in a day. You work there a few weeks, let me know what's going on, then we'll go in and raid the place. Think you two can handle that?"

"Desk clerk?" Daniel said. "Sarge, it was bad enough when I had to drop out of college and take this job. But if my mother hears I'm working as a desk clerk in a hotel, it'll break her heart."

"You're not going to tell her. You're not going to tell anyone. When you're there, you're just an ordinary Joe working as a desk clerk. Not a word to anyone about being a cop. And when you're here, you keep your mouths shut about the hotel. Got it?"

"But how do we know we can get jobs there?" Daniel said.

"It's your lucky day, boys." Callan showed them the ad in the paper. "The Marco Polo Hotel is advertising for two desk clerks. Night shift. Must mean business is pretty good. Go home and put on your good clothes and get over there before anyone else gets the job. Report back to me when you're done."

7.

THE ballroom dancing was Brigid's idea. Or it could have been his mother's. The two had grown so close, they seemed to speak with one voice. Brigid wanted to try to do more of the things she thought Daniel would enjoy. Kathleen assured her he liked dancing.

But Daniel didn't. He'd rather have his teeth filled. Still, he said he'd give it a try.

He hated the slippery polished floor, the wall of mirrors, the awful music. The dance instructor seemed to single them out. He placed Daniel's arm lower down on Brigid's middle. She was so solidly built, it was hard for him to find her waist.

"I thought police officers were good at following orders. Lead with your *right* foot," the instructor said.

The other couples stopped to watch as he tried to lead a reluctant Brigid in a fox trot, while Brigid grimaced and clenched her teeth. Box-stepping their way across the floor, they couldn't seem to catch the rhythm of the song.

"Okay, break everybody," the instructor said. "Punch and cookies on the table. Don't forget the tip jar."

Three dollars for the lessons, another buck for the refreshments. And they were both looking miserable. It was time to tell her he wouldn't be taking any more lessons. He had a new assignment. In fact, he'd be busy most nights.

"But what about dinner to meet Aunt Rose tomorrow? What about taking Peg for ice cream Friday night? And our Saturday night dinner with your mother? Are you saying you're canceling all of them?"

"Afraid so," Daniel said. Maybe there was an upside to working as a desk clerk after all. He paid for two glasses of punch. Brigid drank both.

"I thought you were ready to be done with that job. What about our plans to serve together in Africa? Our life as missionaries helping our brown brothers and sister? What about doing something worthwhile with your life?"

"Being a cop is worthwhile," he said. The only ones who didn't think so were Brigid and his mother. Did he really want to spend the rest of his life with someone just like his mother?

"It would be different if you'd joined the army. Then you'd have something to be proud of."

Brigid knew it was a soft spot. Why would she want to poke it? He was ashamed the little touch of scarlet fever he had as a child had left him deaf enough in one ear so the army didn't want him. The marines wouldn't talk to him. The air force, the navy, all turned him down over a problem he never knew he had. His mother talked so loudly, he didn't realize he was hard of hearing.

The other couples stopped once more to look at them. He saw a dozen faces reflected and multiplied in the wall of mirrors. He and Brigid made a strange, sad couple. Or maybe it was just that stern look on her face when she was forced to have fun.

The music started again. His feet wouldn't move in her direction and she refused to budge.

Brigid kept talking, He'd been leading her on. He'd stolen her heart and tricked her into believing they shared the same vision for their future. He was frivolous and foolish. He was wasting his life. She never wanted to see him again. Not even at church.

The other couples stopped long enough to see her turn away from Daniel on her way out the door.

"Don't forget the tip jar," the instructor called as they left.

8.

FLO placed the small black leather book in the back of the drawer, then locked the drawer. She had to admit, Frank hadn't done badly in bringing Lucy to them. Profits were up, the waiting list was long. And now with Mattie working, there would be nice bonuses for everyone for Christmas. Only maybe not Vera. She wasn't sure about that girl.

Serena Diego called the other day to let Flo know the police paid her a visit and she'd been ready for them. Now she heard someone was giving information to the FBI. In her own theatrical way, Serena swore it wasn't one of hers who was spilling beans, but maybe Flo was the one with a wolf in her henhouse?

It was ridiculous to let Serena make her suspicious. And yet, Flo thought there was something not quite right about the way Vera was acting lately.

"Someone walking on your grave?" Evelyn said.

"What?"

"You just shivered. Then you had the strangest look on your face. Where I come from that means someone's walking on your grave."

"I've got the feeling someone's watching us. You noticed how Vera's kind of strange these days?"

"She's always seemed kind of strange to me. Even for a fussy little white girl." When no one else was around, they slipped back into their own familiar way of talking.

"What do you mean?" Flo said.

Evelyn leaned forward and lowered her voice. "I mean from day one that girl has been looking over her own shoulder. Don't know what's chasing her. But sometimes I think she's looking over my shoulder, too."

"That's what I'm talking about. I've seen her pause a time or two outside the office. I almost feel like she's spying on us. Should we let her go?"

"You know Frank would kill us. He's sweet on her on account of she's the only one who'll do him, if he ever stays awake long enough to do anything."

They put their hands over their mouths to muffle their laughter. Flo had to stop to catch her breath.

"With Lucy here, maybe Frank wouldn't mind so much," Evelyn said.

"Maybe we ought to sit down with Vera. Could be all she needs is some talking."

"You want to be the one?" Evelyn said.

Flo shook her head. "Maybe all she needs is watching."

"Sounds like the best approach to me. She might come to us on her own. Does she know about the books?"

"Funny," Flo said, "I never told her. Told all the others. So, there's no keeping it a secret. But something made me hold back with her."

Evelyn nodded. "You've got good sense even when you don't know you got any sense at all."

"Can't imagine she'd want to do us any harm."

It was Evelyn's turn to feel gooseflesh on her arms. "Now you've gotten me spooked. Maybe it's time to change the code we've been using. Make it something only you and I know. That way if Vera does come snooping around, she won't understand what she's looking at and there won't be anyone here can tell her."

"I like the way you think," Flo said.

Evelyn looked at the photo of Marian Anderson hanging on the wall. She and Flo were among the thousands who heard her sing at the Lincoln Memorial on that Easter Sunday. A historic event. But two years later, nothing had changed; Washington was still split right down the middle as if there were a wall separating white from black.

"In this town," Evelyn said, "you can never be too careful."

9.

ANDREW was ashamed of himself. He'd left Emily alone after the reception. Anything to be done with her baby talk. He was sure Mattie raised her eyebrows every time Emily fussed over him at dinner. Mattie's date—that's a joke—Mattie's escort hadn't seemed to notice. How could she let him touch her?

He paced his office, loosened his tie, unbuttoned his shirt, and for the first time was sorry he didn't keep a bottle of bourbon in his desk.

In truth, if you'd looked at the two women, Mattie in her simple black dress, subtle, elegant. And Emily, her dress cut so low, there wasn't a man in the room who hadn't stopped by to lean over to say hello. Too much make-up, too much jewelry. All tarted up like a—

At least he could still laugh at himself.

But Mattie seemed different. She wasn't the same innocent girl he had met at the Institute. She had a look about her now. A little more sophisticated. The longer she stayed at that place, the more she'd change. He wanted her the way she was when he first saw her.

He could take her away from there; he could marry her. He laughed out loud. His opponents in Michigan would have a field day. His mother might die of shame.

Then what? Set her up in an apartment on Capitol Hill? He heard of colleagues who had those open secrets. But they'd been around long enough, were well-established enough to ride out the bad publicity. It was too hot to think.

If he despised the city throughout the winter, when it was much milder than Michigan, if he felt unhappy with it through spring time, when blooming flowers transformed the town, he'd been told he'd really hate it in the summer, when in spite of Pierre L'Enfant's careful design, the city became a swamp again. The air turned heavy enough to weigh down on him when he stepped outdoors. When he went back inside, he was coated with dust and grime.

Mosquitoes and gnats filled the breezeless evenings. Cloudy skies hid the stars and almost buried the moon. The revolving fan in his office pushed the hot air from corner to corner. The middle of the room felt like an oven.

He tried to work, but there was a strange noise—it sounded like chanting—coming from somewhere beneath his window.

All week, women in black dresses and black veils wailed and wept in the reception areas for the House and Senate. The week before they'd wept in front of the White House. All week, these weeping women—mothers of boys who died in the first war—were crying to keep Congress from extending the draft.

He'd heard about them, but he hadn't seen them. And now, there on the grass in a circle surrounding all of the Capitol, stood those women dressed still in black, each one carrying a lit candle. Hundreds of women, thousands of them, swarming thicker than the mosquitoes, buzzing outside his window. He could barely make out what they were chanting. It sounded like "No more war, no more draft."

If only he could sneak out of his office, get out of the building without having to pass them. Who was he to decide if young men should go to war?

Somehow, he got through the maze of passages and tunnels, back stairs and rear exits, the intricate labyrinth of the House Office Building, and came out beyond their circle. He ran past the cold white marble buildings, the cold white monuments. All seemed tonight like tombs. He kept running, looking back over his shoulder once to spot the next street car. He hopped off in front of the tavern down the block from his apartment.

"Looks like you've seen a ghost," the bartender said.

"Felt like it was mine. Give me whatever you've got on tap and a bourbon chaser. Then give me another round."

"Sounds like it's worse than a woman," the bartender said.

Andrew didn't answer.

"When you got problems that bad, sometimes the only solution is a woman." He lowered his voice, "I know where I can get you one if you don't have one of your own. Dollar fifty, two dollars tops."

Andrew's hand started to shake. "Is that how it's done?"

"Nah. Not for everyone. But you look like a decent sort. Otherwise I wouldn't have mentioned it."

"Thanks." He threw two dollars on the bar. "Keep the change. And keep the woman. I think I know where I can get one on my own."

He called the Franklin Institute. He wasn't sure what to say. He told the woman who answered the phone he'd thrown his back out. He had such terrible pain he couldn't walk. Could they send someone?

The woman on the phone paused. Was he sure he didn't need a doctor? Maybe the emergency room at the hospital?

"No. I know I'm calling the right place. I need someone tonight. As soon as possible."

She hesitated. "This is highly unusual. Have you been referred to us?"

"Look. You know the young woman from Alabama? Tell her I called. Tell her I need to see her."

V.

SUMMER/FALL 1941

1.

IN all his months living in his small Foggy Bottom apartment, Andrew had never noticed the way the lemon-colored light slanted into his bedroom in the mornings. He never paid attention to the birds calling to each other in the trees outside his window. He rolled over and looked at Mattie's face while she still slept. He traced the outline of her chin with his finger, gently touched a golden curl that fell across her ear. She could have been an angel.

Mattie opened her eyes. "A very expensive angel."

"How did you know?"

"You just called me your angel, and I was reminding you I'm pretty expensive for an angel.

He didn't realize he had spoken the words out loud. "Was there anything else I said?"

Mattie sat up in bed, held the sheet tight around her chest. "Last night you were in pretty bad shape. You passed out right after I got here. You looked so unhappy, I didn't want to leave you. Are you feeling better now?"

"Then we, um?" He had so much to drink, he wasn't sure what he dreamed he'd done and what he'd actually been able to accomplish.

She couldn't keep from smiling. "Easiest money I've ever made."

Andrew got out of bed, took his wallet from the top of the dresser, brought it back with him. He opened it and let the bills flutter onto the pillows. "Here, take it. All of it. Then, please, could we never talk of money again?"

Mattie felt pulled in too many directions. She needed the money and hated needing the money. She liked Andrew and hated him. She knew she was on her way to breaking the rule about not falling in love. There was only so much Charlotte and Lucy could teach her—she was still half-country girl in her heart.

She took the handful of bills. Counted off twenty-five dollars—he said it was an emergency. She gave the rest back to him.

"There. Conversation closed."

He hesitated before putting the money back in his wallet. "But what if—"

She shook her head. "I think we passed that turn-off a few miles back."

"How much will it cost to have breakfast with you?"

"Tell you what. I'll call in sick if you do the same. We'll play hooky." She handed him the telephone.

"I can't," he said. "I really shouldn't."

Mattie shrugged. "Suit yourself." She clutched the sheet around her shoulders and went into the bathroom to dress. When she came out he was sitting in his arm chair. He'd taken off his tie, changed his shirt, his jacket was back on the hook. "I've never played hooky in my life," he said. "I got the attendance award five years in a row. You'll have to show me how it's done."

"Me? I won the gold star for attendance eight years straight. Looks like we're both new to this hooky game. How will we know what to do?"

"The blind leading the blind," he said. He closed his eyes and pulled her back into bed.

2.

"TELL me it isn't true," Kathleen said. She still prepared breakfast for Daniel every day, eggs and potatoes, corned beef hash, if they had any leftover. Daniel rarely stopped to eat, always in a hurry to get to work.

"I'll tell you anything you want. But I have no idea what you're talking about."

Kathleen covered her face with her hands. She shook her head. "I can't say it. Can't repeat the filth I heard from Mrs. Casey."

Daniel sat down at the table. Whatever was upsetting her this time, he knew he'd make it easier if he ate the breakfast she prepared. "Tell me what's bothering you. Maybe there's some misunderstanding."

At least that's what he hoped. Hard to believe anyone could have told his mother about his job. He was working in another part of the city. The people in his neighborhood rarely ventured out.

"You know how she is. Dora Casey, pretending the air she breathes is better than anyone else's."

He nodded. For years, his mother and Mrs. Casey had been in a constant competition. He never understood why. Mrs. Casey had four daughters. Each one homelier than the last, Kathleen always said. Mr. Casey, still alive after thirty years of marriage, worked for the water and sewer authority, when he wasn't down at the tavern, drinking away every last bit of his wages. And yet, not a day went by when the two women weren't out on the sidewalk, topping each other's stories, outdoing each other's complaints.

He could see his mother wasn't just putting on a show this time. She was so upset she could barely speak. "Tell me. It can't be that bad."

"Can't it? And wasn't that you Dora Casey saw coming out of the men's bathroom at the National Theatre, clutching a young man in one hand and holding a walking stick in the other?" She was close to tears; her words came out in a rush. "She said there you were dressed in your church clothes, brazen as could be, engaged in sin. Is there any wonder Brigid Ryan tossed you aside?"

"So that's it, is it?" He almost felt relief. At least this one part of his job was public enough to make the newspapers.

"That's all you have to say for yourself? You're seen in public committing an abomination—seen by Dora Casey, no less—and that's all you have to say for yourself? I knew nothing good could come from bringing up a boy without a father. Those uncles of yours aren't worth the time of day."

"Now, Ma, I can explain everything."

He'd been keeping a scrapbook, clippings of news stories about his squad's triumphs. The raids, the arrests, all the small victories in the war on vice. He hid it in the back of his closet, tucked in with his college textbooks.

"Give me a minute, and I'll put all those fears to rest. You'll see for yourself it's not what you're thinking."

He bounded the stairs and returned in minutes with the scrapbook.

"It's my job." He opened the book to the article from the *Washington Star* about the arrests at the National Theatre. It ended with a quote from Police Chief Coker praising the vice squad for all their hard work.

He thought it would make her happy, instead she started sobbing.

"This is how you spend your days and nights? This is what your uncles have gotten you into? I'll kill them with my bare hands."

He never knew how to comfort her when she got this way. He spent his whole life trying to please her. He never had time for friends or girls, sports or hobbies, anything that might take his attention away from her. And still, after all these years of trying, there was nothing he knew to do. She was sure a dark cloud followed her wherever she went. Soon she'd be wailing and cursing the day she was born.

"I thought you'd be proud," he said. "You can tell Dora Casey I was just doing my job. See here where it says we got a commendation from the Chief of Police?"

She blew her nose. "I'll never understand what the good Lord was thinking when he let me be born."

He knew this part by heart. If he told her again it wasn't so bad, she would insist it was even worse. The more he'd comfort her, the louder she'd wail, until she wore herself out. Then she'd pat his head, ruffle his hair, pretend to cuff his ears, and tell him she knew he was trying to do his best. Only it was never enough.

But when he started to say the lines he knew so well, he couldn't say them. Couldn't try to console her. Instead he said, "I don't know why this hurts you so. I'm sorry it does. But it's my job, and I'm good at it." He surprised himself. "If you feel so strongly about it—maybe it's time for me to be living on my own."

He left her with her mouth open, wringing her red and wrinkled hands.

3.

IT was strange for Mattie to hear the sound of her footsteps as she walked across the Institute's marble foyer. She felt as if her feet hadn't touched ground all day. She and Andrew talked as if they'd always known each other, not sure what kept them apart all this time. They were sure they'd spend the rest of their lives together.

No one would have to know about her current job, they agreed. It wasn't as if she'd been doing this for years. It was only a few months. She hadn't done anything, really. Or at least not with that many men. They would put it behind them—she'd go to secretarial school.

There were so many jobs in Washington, she'd be working before she graduated. Or not working. He said he'd be just as happy to have her stay at home, do volunteer work with the other congressmen's wives. It wasn't rushing, was it, for them to be thinking of marriage, and how lucky it was they both wanted four children?

And it wasn't asking too much, was it, for him to expect her to quit the Institute right away? He would understand if she needed another day to find a room somewhere, to say goodbye to her friends.

The noise Mattie's shoes made on the marble floor jarred her. She'd been floating, she'd been flying. She wanted to tell Charlotte. Maybe Lucy and Vera. Eventually Evelyn and Flo.

Charlotte was curled up on her bed with a hot water bottle pressed to her stomach. She looked pale and tired, her hair matted down, her eyes rimmed with red.

"Hey, kid, you look like the cat that swallowed the canary. What are you grinning about?"

Mattie touched Charlotte's forehead; it felt cold and clammy. Her hands were cold, too. "Never mind about me. What's happened to you?"

"It's nothing." Charlotte tried to sit up, keeping the hot water bottle pressed close. She winced each time she moved. "Just a little set back. I should be out of bed in a day or two. On my feet by the weekend."

Flo came into the room carrying a tray with tea and a soft-boiled egg. "How is she?" Flo said to Mattie.

"Look at her. She looks so pale." Mattie held onto Charlotte's hand, still so cold. "She's shivering. What happened?"

Flo signaled for Mattie to step outside. "She lost a lot of blood. Sometimes that happens. It wasn't Doc's fault."

"I don't understand."

Flo started to explain but Charlotte called out to them. "Let me tell her."

Mattie sat back down on the side of the bed. She touched Charlotte's forehead again.

"It's all a question of timing," Charlotte said. "Even good things can happen when you're not ready for them. I know you'd never guess, but I've got one kid already. I can't afford to have another one right now."

"You have a child?" Why was she always so late to catch on to what was really going on?

"Get me my handbag," Charlotte said. "Now take out my wallet. And see there in the back, under all the other stuff, there's a picture of the sweetest little girl in the world. She lives with her grandma, but that's only until I can afford to have her live with me."

Mattie stared at the picture of a little girl with all of Charlotte's features on a much smaller face. "Why didn't you ever tell me?"

Charlotte winced. "Do me a favor, would you? Ask Flo to get a hold of Doc again. I think something's wrong here." She leaned back against the pillow and closed her eyes. "Don't forget, you have to tell me what all your grinning was about. Just let me rest first. Okay?"

Mattie ran for Flo. She was frantic. "Hurry. Please hurry. Shouldn't we call an ambulance?"

Evelyn came out of Flo's office. "Just stay calm," she said to Mattie. "Everything's going to be all right. We've all been through this before. She's going to be fine. Doc will give her another shot and she'll sleep. But, Mattie, honey, you look white as a sheet yourself. Don't go getting sick on us—we need you to help out while Charlotte's not feeling well."

"What? But I can't. Not now. I was going to come in here and tell you—"

"Hush, honey. Whatever it was you were going to tell us will have to wait."

"But," Mattie started to say. She could hear the doctor's footsteps racing down the marble hallway. She could hear the hollow noise of her own footsteps as she raced down the hall after him.

4.

"YOU can't be serious about marrying that girl. You might as well take your career and . . ." John crumpled the cocktail napkin into a ball, kissed the ball and tossed it into the trash bin ten feet away. He'd also been varsity basketball in high school.

"I wish people would stop telling me I don't know what I'm doing," Andrew said.

They were sitting in a green leather booth in the back room of O'Toole's Tavern. John motioned for Andrew to keep his voice down.

"Everyone thinks of you as a loose cannon already. I can't let you do this."

"You're the one who doesn't understand. She's young and innocent. She just fell into this whole ugly business by accident."

John called for the waitress and ordered another round. "If I had a nickel for every time I've heard that story, I'd be able to pick up this tab." He winked at the waitress.

"This time it's true. She's only been at that place for a few months."

"You probably think you can make her respectable. Right?"

"She is respectable. Do me a favor. Meet her first before you make up your mind."

"I'm not sure I want to get involved in this. The three of us? It wouldn't look right."

"What are you afraid of?"

"I've worked hard to keep my nose clean. I can't afford a whiff of impropriety and, by the way, neither can you."

"What if the four of us had dinner?"

"Can't do it. I wouldn't be comfortable being alone with the two of you. Even less comfortable bringing my wife along. You see the problems already?"

"You're making this much harder than it has to be."

"I'm a politician, remember?"

"Tell you what. Why don't I bring her to the reception tomorrow night?"

"The British Ambassador's? Are you sure you understand the consequences?" John shook his head. "Do you know how many important people in this town are regulars at the Institute? Can't you do what everyone else does in your situation—let someone else take her to the reception? Maybe set her up in an apartment, see her whenever you want? Can't you, just this once, stop swimming against the tide?"

"No," Andrew said. "I don't think I can."

5.

DANIEL and Arnold discovered they didn't mind being desk clerks. It kept them off the streets and out of the rain. They'd gathered enough information to raid the Marco Polo Hotel, but they'd been stalling.

Arnold wasn't ready to give up the job. His ulcer was better. He'd been getting some sleep, dropped a pound or two. And on a quiet Tuesday night, with rain keeping customers away, some of the girls might come down from the fourth floor to talk to them. Arnold liked the one named Dawn.

Daniel, grateful for the quiet so he could study his vocabulary building books, was aiming for five new words a day. Not as good as going to college, but it helped pass the time. He sat with Arnold in the little room behind the desk. They both needed to give their feet a rest.

"Supernumerary," Daniel said to Arnold. "Know what that means?"

"Geez, I keep telling you I don't want any new words. I've got more than I can use already."

Outside the hotel, James E. Harris waited impatiently for his driver to come around to open the car door and hold the umbrella for him. He didn't like going out at night in the rain but the tip he received was too good to pass up. The magazine publisher, the one who printed that vile and inaccurate article about him, was said to be in the arms of some tart at the Marco Polo Hotel.

Harris wanted to be there when the man was arrested. He brought along his own photographer. He didn't trust any of the ones from the local papers. Reporters stuck together, protected their own. They'd bury the story.

Daniel and Arnold were in the back room when Harris stormed into the hotel, his driver at his side balancing the umbrella, the photographer walking quickly to keep up.

Harris wouldn't have bothered to stop at the front desk but he wasn't sure if he wanted Room 506 or 508, the ink on the paper had run in the rain. He expected Clint to meet him with the information but Clint wasn't there. Perhaps he'd taken the desk clerks into the back room to interrogate them? Harris pounded on the bell with his fist. "Where's the manager?"

Daniel and Arnold peeked through the opening in the mail slots; it gave them a full view of the front desk. "Must be someone important," Arnold said.

"Don't you know who that is?"

According to Sergeant Callan, Harris was to blame for all the extra hours they had to work. For all the arrests he didn't want to make.

"You go see what he wants," Daniel said. "I'm calling Callan."

"Aw, do you have to? You know he's going to chew us out about something, even if we haven't done anything."

Harris pounded the bell one more time. "Get me the manager."

Arnold straightened his uniform and walked to the front desk. "Can I help you?"

"Let me see the register."

"I'm sorry, I'm not allowed to—" Arnold started to move the register out of reach. Harris grabbed it away from him.

"If you don't cooperate, I'll have you arrested. Now tell me where Victor Marshall is."

"There's no one here by that name," Arnold said. He was starting to shake, his voice cracked.

"Imbecile." Harris reached across the counter and grabbed Arnold by the front of his uniform.

Daniel, with a confidence he never knew he possessed, and a calmness that came to him as a gift, walked up to the front desk. "No need for that. My assistant is not cognizant of the gentleman you referred to. Our guests expect unambiguous anonymity." The vocabulary building must have been working.

"Would you be so kind as to tell me where I can find Victor Marshall?" Harris said, his voice dripping with sarcasm. "Before I throw you two idiots in jail."

"If I might extricate the register?" Daniel held out his hand for the book. "It appears Mr. Marshall is in the Garden Suite, Room 506."

Arnold looked at Daniel with new respect. He swallowed so hard his Adam's apple seemed to get stuck above his collar.

"This way," Harris said to the photographer. He told the driver to wait in the lobby in case Clint showed up. "Be a pity not to share this."

The elevators were old and creaky. One had been stuck on the sixth floor for three years. The other slowly worked its way downward from the fifth floor.

"Take the stairs?" the photographer said.

Harris glared at him. He had his back to the front door and missed Sergeant Callan swinging his nightstick and grinning.

"Well, well, well," Callan said to Harris. "Never thought I'd see you here. Thought you only go to those posh places in New York."

Harris had nothing but contempt for the DC police. He made that clear to everyone.

"I don't recall asking for your help," Harris said.

"Funny," Callan said, "I was going to tell you the same thing. Would you like to explain just what the hell you're doing here?"

The one working elevator ground to a stop at the main floor, the doors gradually opened. Harris and the photographer stepped inside. "No," Harris said, as the doors closed.

"Don't worry, Sarge," Daniel said as Callan watched the elevator ascend slowly. "I gave him the wrong room number."

Callan looked at Daniel. "You did what?"

"Then I called Dawn and let her know Mr. Harris was here looking for Mr. Marshall. She said she'd take him out the back door. I'm afraid Mr. Harris is going to walk in on one of his own men."

"Granger," Callan said, forcing himself to smile, "you surprise me."

Arnold watched in amazement. That was the most praise he'd ever heard Callan give in his two years on the force. "I stalled them, Sarge."

"It's true," Daniel said. "He diverted their attention." Diverted was one of his words yesterday. If he hadn't found a chance to use it, he'd have forgotten it.

The elevator door opened and Harris was shouting before he walked out. "What the devil is going on here?" He walked up to the front desk, tried to reach across for Daniel. "You moron, you incompetent, you . . ."

"Easy," Callan said, "or I'll have to arrest you for assaulting a police officer."

"What? This idiot?" He looked closely at Daniel. "Don't think I'll forget you."

Harris snapped his finger at his driver and waited for him to open the umbrella and raise it over his head before he stepped back into the rain.

6.

CHARLOTTE woke up the second day after her procedure, still in pain. Eyes closed, she groped for the hot water bottle. Mattie woke up as soon as she heard Charlotte moving.

"I'll get that for you," Mattie said.

"How long have you been sitting there, kid?"

Mattie checked her watch. "Couple hours. Not very long."

"Listen. You have to make sure while I'm out of commission you don't let anyone push you around. Don't let them talk you into doing anything you're not ready to do. Okay?"

"You don't have to worry about me anymore. I can take care of myself now."

"Scout's honor?"

"You're the one we've got to keep an eye on."

"Now, what was that good news you were going to tell me? I could use a little something to cheer me up."

Flo stood in the doorway. "Looks like you're almost ready to go dancing."

"Get me a date for tomorrow night and I'll put Ginger Rogers to shame."

"Mattie, honey," Flo said, "could I see you for a minute?"

Mattie looked to Charlotte. "I'll be fine. Just don't forget what I told you," Charlotte said.

Flo raised her eyebrows. "Anything I should know?"

Mattie shook her head.

"Good. Walk with me back to my office."

Mattie was surprised to see Evelyn waiting for them. And Vera. And Lucy. They all stopped talking. Had they already heard she was leaving?

"Look," Flo said, "you know we wouldn't ask you to do anything you don't want to do, but we're in a desperate situation here. Charlotte's a lot sicker than she'll let on. She's going to be in bed for a few weeks. And even after, she might not be able to work. Not right away, anyway."

"Whenever that happens," Vera said, "we all pull together to help each other out."

"If it were you lying in that bed," Evelyn said, "we'd do the same for you."

"But . . ." Mattie said. She promised Andrew she'd tell them all today. Move out as soon as she could. She and Andrew were thinking of a Thanksgiving wedding.

"You know Charlotte," Flo said, "she'd be the last person to ask you for anything. And the first one to help you out. She needs your help."

"But I was planning . . ." Mattie said.

Flo opened the appointment book. "We all have to change our plans. You're the only one with an open schedule. It won't be for long, just a few weeks until we can figure out something else."

"If it's a question of money," Mattie said, "I'll give her whatever I've got."

Evelyn shook her head. "We're all pooling our money but we still won't have enough. Doctor bills, medicine, money for her kid, for her mother. It all adds up to more than we've got."

Mattie looked at Lucy. She remembered all those fifty dollar bills tucked between her breasts.

"Don't look at me," Lucy said. "I put in as much as I could afford. I've got my own family to take care of."

Vera turned her pockets inside out. "I'm broke"

Mattie bit her lip to keep from crying—a tear rolled down her cheek anyway.

"Sweetie." Lucy stood beside Mattie, smoothed her hair. "It won't be so bad. I'll get you through. I've got a dozen more tricks to show you."

Mattie tried to smile. "What am I going to tell Andrew?"

"Andrew?" Flo said. "You didn't see him, did you?"

Evelyn shook her head. "You agreed to marry him, didn't you?"

Flo looked at Evelyn, Evelyn at Vera, Vera at Lucy—they all tried to keep from smiling.

"Oh, honey," Flo said. "You can't marry him. It's completely out of the question. It would ruin him. Besides, you've got a great future here with us."

"Once you get into this business, it's not as easy to give it up as you think," Vera said. "I don't know if I could ever settle down with one guy anymore."

"You're just earning your wings," Lucy said. "Who knows where they'll take you."

"Besides," Evelyn said, with an edge in her voice Mattie never heard before, "you can't walk out on us now. Not after everything we've done for you."

"I'll tell you what," Flo said. "You help us until Charlotte is back on her feet and we'll give you the biggest going away party you've ever seen."

"We'll make it a bridal shower," Lucy said.

"You know Charlotte would do it for you," Vera said.

"I don't know what to say. Can I take a day to think about it?"

"No time to think," Evelyn said. "We need you to fill in tomorrow night. Spencer Voorhees needs an escort for his friend for a reception at the British Ambassador's. That red satin will be perfect."

"But I've already told Andrew I'd go with him," Mattie said.

"Oh, honey," Flo said, "you can't be seen on his arm at an important reception. The gossip columnists would have a field day. They'd have both of you for breakfast. His career would be over by lunch."

"You have to play it safe," Evelyn said. "Let Voorhees protect you and you'll get through all this."

"For now," Flo said, "let's leave things the way they are. It's better for all of us."

7.

"THAT'S it?" Harris said. "A few photographs of Callan with his skinny, washed-out wife?"

Clint nodded. "We've looked everywhere. Not even a little shoplifting when he was a kid. He doesn't drink, doesn't smoke, if he ever gambled we can't find any evidence. He's some sort of zealot."

Harris leaned back in his chair and snapped the band off of one of his special cigars. "I never trust anyone who's that clean. There has to be something. Are you sure he never took a bribe? Never kept any evidence? Never went to a girlie show while he was on duty? Never passed money to a judge?"

"Not one thing." Clint spent three days trying to dig up dirt on Sergeant Callan.

"What about his boss, anything there?"

"Got a sheet a mile long. You name it, he's done it. He's got his fingers in so many pots, you remove him, you'll see holes all over this city."

"Good. We lean hard on Coker—he leans hard on Callan. That promotion he's bucking for? Keep it in front of him until he grovels, then step on him. What else have you got for me?"

Clint shuffled the folders in his lap. "I think you'll like this one." He held open the folder labeled Andrew Stevens. "You know the freshman congressman Voorhees was worried about?"

Vera Hudson, the little call girl they'd had on their payroll for years, was finally earning her keep. She tipped off Clint the minute she heard that Congressman Stevens called the Institute desperate for company.

"Stevens has been seen in the company of one of the women who works at the Franklin Institute." Clint passed along a picture of Andrew and Mattie kissing on the steps of the Lincoln Memorial. He fanned out five more snapshots of the two of them holding hands in a restaurant in Georgetown, walking close to each other down Pennsylvania Avenue, looking in a store window on F Street. One grainy photo, a little out of focus, showed them going into Andrew's apartment building. Another showed them coming out, arm in arm.

"Perfect."

"Wait, there's more." Clint took out a series of photos of Andrew alone inside Boone and Sons jewelers, looking at engagement rings. "Looks like he's thinking of making an honest woman out of her."

"There is a sucker born every minute, isn't there? Who's the girl?"

"Don't know yet. We removed two glasses from Stevens's apartment. We'll see if the fingerprints turn up anything. Should I contact Voorhees with what we've got already?"

Harris blew a smoke ring. He blew a second ring that floated inside the first. He was casting a wider net. Smaller fish were swimming his way already; the bigger fish were sure to follow.

"Let's hold onto these for the time being. Never pays to tip your hand too soon."

8.

ANDREW put his hand in his pocket and felt for the engagement ring. He wanted to give it to her after she met John. It would be a celebration. They'd sip champagne sitting side by side at the small French restaurant in Georgetown where they'd dined two nights ago. He'd slip the ring to her under the table.

He tried to keep it from Betty but she seemed to know he was hiding something. He finally had to show her the blue velvet box, the ring inside. "What do you think?"

"Honestly? I'd be swept off my feet. Hope Emily appreciates it."

"It's not for Emily."

"Did I miss something?"

"Wait till you meet Mattie. You'll see—she's perfect."

"And you've known each other all of, what, three days?" Betty said.

"Ever meet someone and feel like you'd known them all your life?" Andrew said.

And then Betty sighed and stopped her carping because those apple-cheeked Midwestern boys were as corny as any movie she'd ever seen. She left the room to get some tissues. She liked to be alone when she bawled her eyes out over romance.

Betty tried not to eavesdrop while Andrew was on the phone, all she heard was the disappointed silence when he hung up. She heard his chair squeak as he tried to make it swivel. She had to go back in. "Something wrong?"

"She can't make it tonight."

"You've got nothing to worry about. She'd have to have her head examined if she wasn't crazy about you." Betty knew from experience. She'd almost been crazy about him herself, but then she came back to her senses.

"Maybe I ought to cancel."

Betty folded her hands across her chest. "Over my dead body. You know how important it is for you be seen there tonight. The British Ambassador needs all the friends he can get right now. And the President's counting on you to be one of them."

It was hard for him not to smile whenever Betty talked as if his role was crucial to the well-being of the United States. "Call Congressman Winston's office and tell him I'll go with him."

The phone rang just as she reached for it. They both jumped. Both thought it would be Mattie. Both made a face when it turned out to be Emily.

"Andy, love, your Emmy's feeling so neglected she had to go out and buy herself a new dress. You didn't forget our date tonight for the British Ambassador's reception, did you?"

He didn't answer. He was sure he had made it clear they weren't going to see each other anymore. At least that was how he remembered it. Emily, sitting next to him, wearing that ridiculously low-cut green gown, talking baby talk, chattering away. He'd stopped her in the middle of her plans for the rest of their lives, and told her, forcefully, he thought, they weren't right for each other. He was sure he had made it clear.

That wasn't the way she saw it. What she remembered was that he fell into a bad mood after the cocktail party and dinner at the Hotel Washington. Most likely because Emily had been flirting. But she couldn't help herself and he was being silly to pout. She'd given him enough time to get over it.

"Now don't go all quiet on me. I thought you'd have forgiven me by now. I hate it when my sweet little lamb turns into a stubborn mule. If you're going to be grumpy, I think I better catch a ride with Daddy and meet you at the British Embassy. Don't worry. I won't tell him what a silly boy you've been."

9.

VOORHEES and his wife sat across from them in the limousine. "Didn't I tell you she was every bit as fine as one of your own Georgia peaches?" Voorhees said to Bradford Pearson.

Mattie's date was a grabber. He pinched her so hard she was sure she'd have a bruise. He left his greasy fingerprints on her red satin dress. He tried twice to run his hand up Mattie's leg. He leaned so close she could smell his stale breath. Two of his teeth had a greenish cast. White flakes of dandruff dotted the shoulders of his suit. His eyes were already bloodshot and the evening had just begun.

Mrs. Spencer Voorhees looked out the window and ignored her husband. Every time he slapped her on the knee, she turned toward him, then turned away. She slowly sipped her bourbon, occasionally dipping her index finger into her glass to swirl the ice cubes.

Mattie watched it all, horrified, and tried to pretend she was somewhere else. But then a hand would creep up under the hem of her dress and she'd be drawn back into the backseat of a limousine, on her way to a reception at the British Embassy.

It was the most important embassy in town ever since the President came up with a way to help his closest allies without getting directly into the war. In one of his radio chats he explained the United States would only be lending the British the equipment they needed. The same way you'd help a neighbor if his house was on fire and he didn't have a garden hose, but you did. A simple, neighborly helping hand, the President said.

And now everyone wanted to weigh in on what they thought the British Ambassador should do with all that help.

"Tell me the truth about this Lend-Lease deal," Bradford Pearson said when he was introduced to the British Ambassador. "You boys really going to return all that equipment when you're done?"

Voorhees, still sober enough to note the Ambassador's discomfort, peeled his friend away from the receiving line.

"You don't want to waste your time talking business when you've got this fine young lady just waiting for you to ask her to dance, do you?" Voorhees said to Pearson.

Pearson's hands were clammy on her back. His breath sourer than before. She could smell the sweet pomade he used on his hair. It mixed in with the strange scent of the wax he used on his mustache. And all the time he danced with her, he kept stepping on her feet. She was afraid to look at her satin pumps to see how badly they'd been scuffed.

"I hope you'll excuse me," she said. "I'm afraid I've got a terrible headache. I think I need to sit down."

She wove her way through the crowded dance floor, headed for the few empty seats near the door. She felt sick to her stomach. The room was hot. Her date was awful. How could Charlotte stand all this? How could she?

"You set a bit, darlin', and I'll get you something to drink. Can't have you passing out on me while the night is still so young." Bradford Pearson lurched back through the crowd, trying to find one of the bars.

She put her head in her hands and waited for the room to stop spinning. The band seemed to be playing inside her left ear.

"You're here," Andrew said. "But I thought you said you had something important tonight."

She looked up at him. With the noise and the heat and the pounding in her head, she couldn't think of what to say.

"I don't understand." Andrew clutched at the ring box still in his pocket.

"I can explain." She tried to stand, almost lost her balance, steadied herself on the back of the chair.

"I should hope so," John said, walking up behind Andrew with two drinks in his hand. "I'd feel like a cad if I'd forgotten to get you a drink." He held out a highball for Andrew, held out his free hand to Mattie. "You must be Mattie. I've heard so much about you. I'm delighted you could join us after all."

She smiled weakly. "I'm very pleased to meet you, too. But I'm afraid I've got this terrible headache. I need to get to the ladies' room. If you'll excuse me for a minute, I'll be right back."

"Of course," John said. "Andrew, do you think you ought to accompany her?"

"Now hold on a minute," Bradford Pearson said. "We've got a name for fellas who try to sneak another man's gal when his back is turned."

"There's my naughty Andy." Emily pushed her way through the crowd to grab his arm. "I thought you stood me up, you silly boy."

"Mattie?" Andrew looked from her to Bradford Pearson.

Mattie looked back at him, at Emily clutching his arm, at Bradford Pearson, with his greenish teeth and his bloodshot eyes, at John Winston and Spencer Voorhees all crowding around. She picked up the skirt of her red satin dress and ran out of the room.

10.

THE jelly donuts had been replaced with glistening grapefruit halves dotted with sugar and fat baked apples covered in cinnamon. Fresh biscuits filled a silver basket. There was oatmeal in a large, blue bowl for anyone who wanted it. But everyone was quiet at breakfast waiting to see if Mattie would appear. They'd all heard her crying in the shower.

"I won't say I told you so," Evelyn said.

"Good. Because I don't want to hear it," Flo said.

"This is my fault," Charlotte said. "If I hadn't gotten sick, none of this would have happened. I've got to make it right."

"No," Flo said. "Wait until she comes to you. She'll sort this out."

"You know as well as I do the men in this town can turn your head so fast you can't think straight," Evelyn said. "Maybe Charlotte can talk some sense back into her."

"It's okay," Mattie said, showered and dry-eyed. "I don't need sense, just a little courage." She took the empty chair next to Charlotte. "Why isn't anyone eating?" She took one of the baked apples, poured thick cream down the center. "My momma used to make this all the time for me."

Charlotte handed her a napkin to catch the tear rolling down her check.

"That's it. You're coming with me," Charlotte said. "We'll figure this out."

Together they asked Sam to schedule an appointment later in the day with Congressman Stevens.

Charlotte coached Mattie all morning. "A clean break. Like ripping off a bandage. Just do it all at once."

Mattie tried to smile. She probably had the shortest engagement on record. It didn't last long enough for him to give her a ring. She didn't have a chance to tell her momma and Aunt Lil. She hadn't even had enough time to get over being in love with him.

"Don't let him sweet talk you out of it," Charlotte said.

Andrew wasn't like that. Was he? "Maybe there's still a chance we could move away. Start over."

Charlotte threw her hands up in the air, gave an exaggerated sigh. "Kid, we've been through all that. You know this is for the best. Now chin up, shoulders back. Go in there, and show him what you're made of."

She was more nervous than she'd been the first time she met him. She didn't need Charlotte to tell her she had to be the one to break it off. She just couldn't let herself look in those kind blue eyes.

Mattie opened the door to the private sitting room and there was Andrew with his head lowered. He seemed to be muttering to himself, rehearsing what he was going to say.

"Can I get you a drink?" Mattie said. "Some coffee?"

"No thank you," Andrew said automatically. Then he looked up. "Oh, it's you. I'm glad you called. Look, I wanted to tell you—"

"Wait, before you say anything, I need you to know—" She was afraid whatever he had to say would get her crying again and she'd done enough of that.

"I've got to get this off my chest," he said.

"But first I want to clear the air," she said. Hadn't she and Charlotte gone over all the choices and wasn't there really only one that made any sense?

He interrupted her. "What I'm trying to say—"

She interrupted him. "If you'd just listen a minute—"

But he couldn't. "It'll be easier if I—"

She held her index finger to his lips, "Hush a moment. I hate to have to say this, because I really do like you, but—"

"It's over," they both said at once.

"What?" she said.

"Did you just say what I think you said?"

And they both started laughing, quietly at first, then louder. Andrew doubled over and Mattie wiped tears out of her eyes.

Sam stood in the doorway. "Everything okay in here, Miss Mattie?"

"We're fine, Sam," she said, gulping for air. "We're just fine."

She looked at Andrew. They both grew quiet. And then it was awkward all over again.

"This time, hear me out," he said. "I've never known anyone like you. I wish I'd met you anywhere but here. If there were some way we could run off together—make everything else disappear—I'd do it. But John's right, I've got to grow up sometime. I've put it off too long."

"You just may be the nicest man I've ever met." She took his right hand, held it between both of hers. "You deserve a lot of happiness. And if our paths ever circle back and the timing is right. If I ever do leave here and make a name for myself. Well, let them try and stop us from seeing each other."

He traced the outline of her nearly perfectly heart-shaped face one last time.

"It's bad luck to say goodbye," Mattie said. "So, Godspeed." She kissed him on the cheek.

"Don't take any wooden nickels," he said.

Andrew turned to leave, turned around again and grabbed her, kissed her hard on the mouth.

Mattie held a finger to his lips. "Not another word."

VI.

WINTER/
SPRING 1942

1.

THE bombing of Pearl Harbor really did change everything. The whole city went from silly to serious on a Sunday afternoon.

Andrew was on his way to Union Station when he heard the news. It felt as if the city itself had been bombed. Radios blared. Cars stopped. People walked around looking dazed. They gathered at each of the monuments. They huddled near the churches. No one knew where to go. *If they could bomb us in Hawaii, where will they hit us next? Is any place safe anymore?*

He rushed Lorraine to her train. Everyone said the trains were still running but didn't know for how long. She wanted to get back home to her family in Muskegon.

Lorraine was the one who suggested the visit. She wrote him to say she was sorry she let him slip away. Could he forgive her?

His old loneliness had crept back in. He said he'd be happy to see her again. But it didn't seem to matter now.

Lorraine cried when she said goodbye. Everyone at the train station was crying. *Who knows if the whole word is going to blow up in our face?*

"I'll write," he said. But he wasn't sure he meant it. He wasn't sure of anything.

He went straight from the train station to his office. Many of the other congressmen did the same. They milled around all afternoon waiting for information. *How could we not strike back now? Is there anyone left who doesn't want us in the war? Are we now fighting with the Japanese? What about the Germans? What about the Italians?* The Capitol was full of questions and accusations, but no one had any answers. He left when word came the President would address them all the next day.

The President did what they all expected—he declared war. Andrew contacted his draft board. He was ready to leave as soon as they needed him.

When he met John a month later, John's hair had turned white. It happened overnight, after his son joined the navy and headed out to the Pacific.

"You're having another one of your crazy ideas," John said over lunch. "Let them assign you to the Pentagon. Even if you and I know you don't have enough intelligence to take care of yourself, you could fool them into giving you an intelligence job right here." He'd started to drink heavily; it showed on his face. "Besides," John raised his glass of wine, "I can't afford to lose you both." He'd grown a little sloppy and sentimental. "You know you're like a son to me, too. I'd hate like hell to see you in combat. Look how badly you did under fire with your own party. Take a desk job."

Andrew's father would have hauled him off by his collar and taken him down to the draft board in Muskegon. *Any man who can't serve his country, can't be good for anything else,* he would have said. His mother pleaded with him to stay home. Betty accused him of running away.

"Your responsibility is here," Betty said. "People are counting on you."

He hated to admit he'd made a terrible mess of everything. Why shouldn't he run away? He started drinking too much himself. Secretly. A flask in his desk he was sure Betty hadn't discovered. A few too many drinks with John at lunch. A stop at the tavern on his way home from work. He'd grown a small paunch.

Spencer Voorhees didn't mince words. "Boy," he said, after their last committee meeting, "you are looking the worse for wear. Best thing you could do for yourself is go right into the army and let them get you back into shape. With the kind of friends you've got here, we can make sure your life isn't too hard. You'll come back a war hero. Nothing the ladies like better than a man with medals. Wouldn't hurt your career none, either." He slapped Andrew on the back. "What do you say? Want me to set you up with a desk job?" Voorhees acted as if he'd arranged the war himself.

"Just say the word," Voorhees offered again.

"Thanks," Andrew said, "I can manage on my own."

"Can you now? Word around town is you've been scraping bottom lately. Might do all of us a favor by taking a little *high-ay-tus*. If you catch my drift."

He understood much too clearly. The head of the Democratic party wanted him out of the way. They had a new man in Kalamazoo lined up to take his place.

"You get that gal of yours to let my office know when you're shipping out, hear? We'll give you a proper send-off."

2.

AT first, after Pearl Harbor, everyone was too afraid to leave the apartment building. They were sure Washington would be the next target. Who ever heard of Pearl Harbor?

Business slowed to a crawl. When it picked up again, everyone was jittery. No one knew anymore who they could trust. Was any place safe? Was everyone being shipped overseas, or did it just feel like it?

By February, Flo insisted they all needed to get out. They would take a trip to Virginia for Charlotte's daughter's fourth birthday. Mattie bought and wrapped all the presents. Vera made the cake. Evelyn brought a package of balloons saved from a New Year's Eve party two years ago. Lucy was off in New Jersey visiting her family.

On the first Saturday, they closed the Institute for the day. Charlotte, still thin and pale, was grateful for the company. She was nervous about seeing her daughter again after all these months.

Mattie sat next to Charlotte on the bus. Flo and Evelyn in the seat across from them. Vera took the one closest to the driver.

"I hope she still recognizes me," Charlotte said.

"Of course, she will," Mattie said. But Charlotte had changed so much, she didn't look the same. Neither did Mattie.

"The two of you could use a trip to the country," Flo said. She turned in her seat to look at them. "We've got to do a better job of feeding you both."

Evelyn tapped the straw basket she carried in her lap. "Fried chicken, biscuits, and a homemade cherry pie."

"And a birthday cake," Vera said.

The bus ran smoothly across the Memorial Bridge but when they reached Virginia, the driver pulled over to the side of the road and stopped. He turned around and looked at Flo and Evelyn. "Virginia state line," he said and waited.

Evelyn lifted her basket off the seat and carried it with her as she and Flo moved down the aisle towards the back of the bus. They took two seats by the back door.

"What in the world is going on?" Mattie said.

"Negroes can't ride in the front of the bus in the state of Virginia," the driver said. "Those two thought they could pass, but I know better. I've been driving this line for eight years." He shook his head. "Don't know why they don't make it easy on themselves and sit back there in the first place." He eased the bus back into traffic.

"I never knew," Mattie said to Charlotte.

"Change anything? Being from the South and all."

"Of course, it does." Mattie played up her accent, pretended to fan herself, like Scarlet O'Hara. "Where I come from, a Southern lady always sits with her friends." She followed Flo and Evelyn to the back of the bus. Vera and Charlotte followed her.

ELIZABETH Marie didn't care if her mother was skinny as a rail and pale as a ghost. She was so happy to see her, she almost knocked Charlotte down when she ran into her arms. She greeted each of the women with a handshake, a curtsy, and a kiss on the cheek.

Charlotte's mother banged around the small dark kitchen in the back of the townhouse in Arlington. They could hear her slam the kettle on the stove. They could hear her rattle the plates as she put them on the pine table. "I suppose you and your *lady friends* will want some tea," her mother said to Charlotte. The way she said the word lady let them know she didn't think they were.

"We've brought cake," Vera said.

"Let me see, let me see," Elizabeth said, tugging on Vera's dress.

Vera managed to get butter, eggs, and squares of milk chocolate from one of her regulars. He sneaked them cigarettes and nylons and enough sugar and coffee to last them through the year.

Evelyn opened the basket so Elizabeth could see the fried chicken and biscuits, the crisscross crust of the cherry pie.

. "Charlotte," her mother said, "can I see you in the kitchen a minute?" She didn't wait until Charlotte closed the door to start arguing.

"I'm not a fool. I can just imagine how you got all that food."

Elizabeth climbed onto Mattie's lap. "Tell me a story. Please." Mattie started to tell her about the three bears but she couldn't speak loudly enough to drown out the argument in the kitchen.

"You bring them here? To my house? To visit your own daughter? What kind of a mother are you?"

"A better one than you were."

"You think I don't know what you were sick with all these weeks?"

"Goldilocks tried the first chair and it was too hard," Mattie said.

"And the second one was too soft," Elizabeth said. "What was my mommy sick with?"

"Who do you think pays for everything?" Charlotte said.

"Why don't we have our picnic now?" Flo said. "And then you can open your presents and we'll have cake."

"Does mommy pay for everything?" Elizabeth said.

"Look what I've got for you." Evelyn pulled the package of balloons from her purse. She blew up a red balloon as big as a basketball. She tossed it to Elizabeth.

"Don't expect me to sit down with them," Charlotte's mother said. "I'm a good Christian woman."

"Can we have the cake first?" Elizabeth said.

"Tea is ready." Charlotte carried a tray into the living room. She put on her best smile when she heard the front door slam. "My mother needs to go to the store to pick up a few things. I like to give her a break whenever I can get out here."

"Is Grandma mad at you?"

Charlotte bent down to scoop up Elizabeth in her arms. "Grandma's not mad, sweetie, she's tired."

"Can we have the cake first?" Elizabeth said again.

"That is such a good idea. I bet if we save a big piece for Grandma, she'll be much happier when she gets back."

Elizabeth picked up her piece of cake in her hands. She got white icing on her face, her fingers, and all over Charlotte's hair when she reached up to kiss her mother.

"Hold it." Vera snapped the perfect picture of them smiling.

3.

IN the year since he let Daniel join the force, Sergeant Callan's vice squad had grown from a handful of men to a battalion of forty. But every time Callan shut down a call house, two more would open. Last time anyone counted, there were more than fifteen hundred prostitutes operating in the District of Columbia. On his watch. Most of them amateurs, small-time operators, in and out of jail faster than they could turn a trick.

And that fat bastard Harris was still trying to move in on his territory. It was federal land, Harris argued. Anyone committing a crime was breaking federal laws. He was a conniving con man who would have spied on his own mother in the bathroom if he thought it would help his career. He was building an empire and everyone was so busy worrying about the war, no one tried to stop him. Except Callan.

Callan got into hot water a few months back over the fiasco at the Marco Polo Hotel. The Chief came down hard on him. Too hard. He was sick and tired of being everyone's favorite punching bag. That's why he went behind the Chief's back to set up surveillance at the Franklin Institute, the high-class operation on Connecticut Avenue. He had Burns and Granger out there every day. Two of his other men were there every night. It was a tricky assignment. They didn't want to arouse the suspicions of the respectable people who lived in the fancy apartment building.

Callan had almost enough evidence to raid the place, but he didn't want to rush it. The right time would come. He had photos of men going in and out of the building. Photos of some of the women. Unless he could get his hands on the books, he'd have a hard time getting convictions. He needed to prove money was changing hands for all those "health-giving benefits" before he could lock them up. Sure, it was against the law to give a member of the opposite sex a massage, but who would care if he caught a woman rubbing a man's back?

That Institute operated right down the street from the National Zoo. A place where families went on weekends. Ought to be enough to put them in jail, but in this crazy world a cop had to be more careful than a criminal. Lately Callan had the feeling his office was bugged. He suspected Harris put a tap on his phone. He tried to tell the Chief and the Chief told him he might need a long vacation. Was it his imagination or was it possible the Chief was working with Harris, too?

4.

DANIEL never thought of his job as dangerous. Ever since the war had started and most of the men he knew were getting drafted, he was a little embarrassed at how easy his job was. Most of the time.

Now he was up against a new and different kind of danger. He had a crush on one of the women he was supposed to be watching. Hard to believe she worked there, but he was sure she did. Sometimes, he spotted her going out, arm-in-arm with a man old enough to be her father. Other times the fellas were more his own age.

Callan warned them—delivered a full sermon on the subject—they were not ever to get involved with any of the women they hoped one day to arrest.

It wasn't just about breaking the law, Callan told them, it was about diseases so awful you'd wish you'd been sent to fight on the frontlines instead.

Standing out there every day, trying to keep his mind off the young woman with the pretty face, he went over every word he memorized in the six-volume vocabulary building books.

Sometimes, when she came out, she smiled at him. Once he was sure she mouthed the word hello.

He was afraid one day he might go right up and start talking to her.

5.

TWICE Mattie thought about stopping to talk to the young man with the blond hair waiting outside her building. He always smiled and nodded hello each time she passed, as if he knew her. He looked like the brother of a friend or someone she knew back home. He was usually talking with that other man, the short, heavy one.

She'd seen the two men leaning against the wall across the street, eating popcorn. The blond one looked so familiar, it made her homesick. Then she'd catch herself. No sense in thinking about home—it would be a long time before she could go back. How could she show up looking the way she looked now? Her momma would read her face and know right away the kind of big city life Mattie had been living. She'd wait a while. Move out over Easter. Get a job with . . . she'd cross that bridge when she got to it. A few of her clients offered to help her find work. Charlotte had a friend who was willing to share her room in a boarding house on Wisconsin Avenue, right near the trolley. Flo said she'd been saving some money just for Mattie, for a bonus. Vera gave her a real leather suitcase so she could throw out that cardboard one she had brought with her all those months ago.

The war talk was everywhere now, but it seemed to slip into the background for a few hours one fine day in March, giving Mattie just enough time to walk out of her building, walk right past Daniel, on her way to the zoo. She could have sworn she saw him trying not to let her see he was looking at her.

It was almost spring and the zoo animals were courting each other, and if the war was all that mattered, you couldn't tell it on the faces of the children leaning over the rail to feed the elephants peanuts. Or the parents pushing prams near the pen where they kept the zebras. Or the vendors selling hot dogs and ice cream.

She stopped to buy a box of Cracker Jacks and bumped right into the young man she'd seen earlier.

"Excuse me," Daniel said, his face turning red.

"If I didn't know better, I'd think you were following me. Seems like I keep seeing you everywhere I go."

His face turned even redder. He tried to speak but nothing came out.

"It's all right." Mattie touched his arm. "I was just kid-ding."

Daniel could have kicked himself for acting like such a fool, but she did leave him tongue-tied.

"I bet you live near here, too," she said. "That must be why I see you all the time."

He couldn't believe she'd noticed him. The one woman he watched more carefully than the others. The one who slipped into his dreams. He often imagined talking to her, displaying his large new vocabulary, surprising her with his erudition. And here she was and he was speechless.

"No, wait." Watching him struggling to speak, Mattie couldn't resist teasing him. "I bet it's the zoo you like, right? That's the reason I see you around here so much."

"Ma'am," Daniel said. "You can see right through me with those pretty eyes of yours." *Ma'am?* She probably wasn't any older than he was.

"You wouldn't care to walk around with me, would you?" She'd been feeling lonely and homesick and, after all these months, suddenly lost in Washington. "I'd be grateful for the company."

Funny, with all the things she'd done in the past year, asking him to take a walk with her felt the most brazen. How could she have been so forward? Mattie knew better than anyone just because you were attracted to a person, didn't mean they liked you back.

Arnold, heavier now from the doughnuts and popcorn and Cracker Jacks that kept him busy while he watched the Franklin Institute, came huffing up the path. He cleared his throat. "Can I speak to you?" he said to Daniel. "Alone."

Mattie backed away. "I'm sorry I bothered you. I can see you're busy."

She was blushing now herself. "It was nice meeting you."

She walked straight down to the elephant house, not understanding for one minute why she felt so much like crying.

6.

HARRIS looked through the photos one more time. He glanced at the one of Voorhees—the image of the man undressed was in and of itself more obscene than anything else on his desk. He rifled through the rest of the photos. Most of the men looked familiar. That pleased him. What didn't please him was the lack of solid evidence they needed to raid the Franklin Institute.

They'd already shut down the place run by that South American madam, caught a few diplomats, no one important, and she was shipped back home to Argentina. But the Franklin Institute, with its powerful clientele, was more along the lines of what he wanted. He needed more evidence.

Harris looked at the photos again—something bothered him. He started to go through the pile one more time when Miss Dunstan knocked. "The seventh-grade class from Keokuk, Iowa, is here."

He barely had time to put away the pictures before the students entered his office. "Well, well, well." He stood up and tried to smile as the group of students filed in behind Clint. "Looks like we have our next crop of crime fighters."

"We're so excited to be here," the teacher said. "I can't tell you how many of my students think of you as their hero."

Clint cleared his throat. He tried to signal to Harris he'd left his desk drawer open. A black-and-white photo of a man and young woman, in a position most likely not known to the seventh graders of Keokuk, Iowa, was very visible. The woman in the photo looked young, maybe too young. Clint tried to look away, then looked back again. There was something not quite right there, but he couldn't place it.

Clint cleared his throat again. "Now that you've met the man who is an inspiration to us all," he stood in front of Harris's desk, trying to block their view, "why don't I take you down to the fingerprint lab."

The students buzzed to each other, a few clapped their hands.

"Oh, but won't you just say a few words to the class?" the teacher asked Harris. "It would mean so much to them."

Harris waited for Miss Dunstan to bring in the photographer. No sense wasting his time with a bunch of schoolchildren if they didn't make good use of it.

"We've made a gift for you," the teacher said. She held up a blue-ribbon badge, the kind they gave out at the County Fair, with the words "Public Citizen Number One" written on it in gold.

"Remember," Harris said. "Work hard. Keep your nose clean. And always be true to your country and the principles on which it was founded."

Harris stood in the middle of the group, the teacher to his right, handing him the blue ribbon, while the photographer captured the moment and Clint, his hip to the desk drawer, hid the snapshot of the Honorable Congressman Voorhees hard at work for his country and the principles on which it was founded.

7.

LUCY wanted to try out her new Easter outfit. With the war on, she'd been lucky to find a silk suit that fit and flattered her. She didn't even want to think about what she had to go through to get the hat with the small lacquered cherries that framed her face. She wanted to break in her new shoes. And she just wanted to get out of the apartment. She was going stir crazy after being in bed for two weeks with the mumps. She volunteered to be the one to run down to the corner market to pick up a loaf of bread.

"Keep me company," she pleaded with Mattie. "I don't know what's come over me, but I hate to be alone these days."

Mattie had been feeling the same way all week. How could she say no?

"Don't turn around," Lucy whispered, slipping her arm through Mattie's and laughing, "but I think we're being followed. There's a cute blond guy who can't seem to take his eyes off of us." She swung her hips a little, the way she used to when she was an artiste at Minsky's.

Mattie turned in time to catch Daniel's eye. He nodded at her and looked as if he might speak, but then his friend took him by the arm and held him back.

"My, oh, my," Lucy said, "would you look at that." She pointed to the handsome man walking toward them. "Wouldn't kick him out of bed in a rainstorm," she said as Clint strolled by.

"Strange," Mattie said, "I know I've seen him around here before, too." She shivered.

"What's wrong with you?" Lucy said. "The sun is shining; the birds are singing. We've got our health and the clothes on our back. Like the Reverend Peale says, you have to stay positive."

Mattie was positive. She was sure the world was coming to an end. Her father had been slowly and painfully killed by the last war. The only thing that had kept her momma going all these years was the belief his death had meant something. He died to make sure there'd never be any more wars. Why was everyone so happy to send men off when it might not make any difference? Why were they having a going away party for some friend of Voorhees's when whoever it was might come home wounded or never come back at all?

Lucy paid for the bread, bought a pack of Camels and two pieces of bubble gum. She flirted with the man behind the counter. His son had dropped out of high school to join the marines. He'd be heading to the South Pacific soon. His father was worried he'd be missing out on an education.

"You be sure and send him to see me before he leaves, George," Lucy said. "I'll teach him he can't always trust what he learns in those training films."

Arnold scribbled on a small white pad, his fingers sticky with chocolate from the Powerhouse candy bar he'd half-eaten while he was waiting his turn in line.

"Let's have some fun," Lucy said. She nodded in the direction of Arnold Burns.

Mattie wasn't unhappy to find herself left alone with Daniel.

8.

"YOU say she's how old?" Callan said.

"Aw, Sarge," Arnold said, starting to doubt his own memory under Callan's questioning. "I can't say for sure, but I know I got an eighteen-year-old cousin who looks twice her age. Shame to see a young girl like that out on the street."

Daniel kept quiet. He'd sworn he wouldn't mention the half hour Arnold was gone. Or the way he talked about Lucy for the rest of the day. Arnold wanted them to take up their post an hour earlier so they could catch her on the way to the store again. But Callan summoned them. He wanted a full report, otherwise he'd pull them off the assignment and give it to someone else.

Arnold swore he never would have mentioned Lucy if it hadn't meant losing that assignment.

"Cute kid," Arnold said.

Callan raised his eyebrow.

"My cousin, I mean," Arnold said.

"I don't give a fat policeman's ass about your cousin. Tell me more about the girl."

Daniel could see the sweat start to pour off of Arnold's face. He'd grown accustomed to his partner's personal habits in the weeks they'd spent on surveillance. Indigestion from greasy crullers. A case of athlete's foot he couldn't shake. Dry scalp that drove him crazy in the winter. Perspiration that poured off him whenever he was nervous. And Arnold was nervous whenever he talked to Sergeant Callan.

"Came down from New Jersey?" Callan said.

"Said some guy paid her a bundle to take a ride with him." Arnold didn't mention how Lucy took his hand and placed it under her blouse to show him where Frank had slipped in all those bills. "Brought her here and left her with a couple of old broads in that fancy apartment building on Connecticut. She said they made her do things she never wanted to do."

Callan looked at Daniel for agreement. It wasn't the same story Arnold had told him. Arnold said there wasn't anything Lucy didn't want to do. Daniel nodded at Sergeant Callan. He didn't care what Arnold said about Lucy, as long as he didn't mention Mattie. In the back of his mind, he was making his own plans.

"I knew it," Callan said. "Underage and forced on the streets. Might be all we need. Might be a promotion waiting for all of us."

Arnold didn't want to tell the Sarge about the party Saturday night. He was hoping he could sneak in there on his own time.

But Callan had a way of wearing Arnold down. In the end, he told Callan everything Lucy told him. About the Franklin Institute and the women who lived there. About the crazy drunk who owned the place but lived in New York. About the famous men she met and the money she made. He told Callan every last detail, except he never told him about that tongue trick he was hoping he could teach his wife to do the way Lucy did it.

9.

ANDREW'S orders told him to report to Fort McNair on the first of April. He never knew he'd made so many friends in Washington until it came time to say goodbye to all of them. Betty was still bawling her eyes out. She checked with some astrologer and clairvoyant and learned Andrew was born under a lucky star. But Betty had seen enough movies to know even a lucky star couldn't keep him safe in a foxhole.

Emily took time out from her work at the Office of Civilian Defense to coo at him and tell him how much she'd miss him, even though they hadn't seen each other in months. She told him it would be foolish to wait for him, given how naughty he'd been to her, but she was silly enough to try. She gave him a lock of her hair to take with him overseas.

Lorraine said she couldn't make the trip to see him off, but she'd write every day. She knew he'd come home to her.

John raised his glass and told Andrew he and his wife would save a place for him at their Thanksgiving table next year. They expected to see him all in one piece. Did he like dark meat or white?

Andrew thought about calling Mattie. Thought about it two, three times a day, but never knew what he'd say. He walked by the building once but didn't go in. He waited, thinking somehow he could wish her there. When she didn't appear, he walked back downtown and donated a pint of his blood to the Red Cross.

Voorhees acted as if he were losing his one true friend in life. "In spite of myself, I've come to like you, boy. You got what we call integrity and you don't find enough of it in this town." He insisted Andrew be his guest on Saturday night at a little shindig he was throwing. A party in Andrew's honor. A way to show his appreciation for all the boys in uniform. He wanted it to be a surprise. Not even Betty knew where Voorhees was taking him.

If there was anything good about leaving, it was that he didn't have to worry about Voorhees any more. If he didn't want to show up on Saturday, he didn't have to. His father was right. The army was making a man out of him.

10.

"I don't like it," Evelyn said. "We've never given a party here before. It's just asking for trouble."

Spencer Voorhees, looking for any excuse to spend time at the Franklin Institute, was throwing the party for Andrew there. The boy had been a thorn in his side ever since he'd come to Washington. Was it so odd for Voorhees to celebrate his going?

"We'd be better off going down the street to the Shoreham," Evelyn said. "Why bring a bunch of strangers here?"

Flo took out the small black leather ledger. "We need the money. See for yourself."

Evelyn had devised a new way to keep the books—they now used a code. Ever since the police and the FBI declared their own war on vice in Washington, sent Serena Diego off to Argentina, and arrested some of her employees, Flo and Evelyn tried to do a better job protecting themselves, the women who lived with them, and the other dozen or so around town they called on when business was good. Lately, the women sometimes wore disguises, long trench coats over their cocktail dresses. Often, they hopscotched their way to a meeting, going first to the wrong address in case they were being followed. And they used a simple code to keep track of their money. The first ten letters of the alphabet stood for the numbers one through ten.

Business had been good during the past year. Their accounts filled three of the small black leather books they kept hidden in the locked drawer in Flo's office.

Evelyn paged through the most current book. "We can manage. I've got a bad feeling about this party. Got a bad feeling all around. I've been having bad dreams."

"It's just war worries," Flo said. "Everyone's having send-off parties these days. We'll be doing our patriotic duty. Also, we'll be keeping Spence Voorhees happy. The way things are going, he might end up being the only man left in town. We can't afford to lose his business."

"If he's going to do all his entertaining here, I'm not so sure we can afford to keep it, either." Evelyn hadn't told Flo yet about her decision to leave. She was going back home to help her sister raise her four kids. She had bought a bus ticket to Atlanta for the Monday after the party.

"You worry too much. Besides, I promised Mattie we'd see her off in style. Hate to lose her." Flo fiddled with the papers on her desk to keep from looking at Evelyn. She knew her old friend and business partner would see she was starting to cry.

"Everything's changing so fast," Evelyn said. "Sometimes I think nothing will ever be the same again."

VII.

NOVEMBER
1945

1.

I
F Washington after the war was going to have any rules, James E. Harris was going to be the one to make them. It pleased him when all the pieces fell into place.

Most of his old enemies had died, retired, or been run out of town. And the ones who remained? He caressed the black leather cover of the book he held in his hands. Two identical books were inside the locked top drawer of his desk.

The books were in his possession thanks to his uncanny knack for knowing when to be at the right place at the right time. It was his particular genius for sensing scandal that led him to send his agents to the Franklin Institute that Saturday night three years ago.

The same night his men in New York picked up Frank Billings, the alcoholic owner of the Institute. Guilty of transporting underage women across state lines for immoral purposes as well as his own pleasure. It was not surprising Harris's men caught Billings in the arms of a teenager. Billings and all his employees were arrested for conspiracy to violate the Mann Act.

It saddened him to turn over the women in the apartment to that imbecile police sergeant, but Callan insisted on handcuffing them and loading them into the paddy wagon in front of all the neighbors. Callan posing like a peacock for the newspaper reporters.

Harris let Callan have his moment. But he'd never get promoted. Harris knew about the secret trysts Callan's men arranged with some of the women at the Institute.

And feeling magnanimous, it had been easy for Harris to let a stunned Spencer Voorhees flee before the flashbulbs popped. One picture of his skinny white legs and his thin black socks was all Harris needed to remind Voorhees of his debt during the coming years.

He knew better than anyone it was his cunning alone, and not the tip from Vera Hudson, that made it possible to locate and secure the three small black books hidden in the desk of Flo Maxwell. All written in a code a child could decipher. If he had not been able to explain to Flo the serious damage she might cause to her family—whose influence in Louisiana would surely be diminished—he might never have been able to convince her to become the state's witness. Then the trial itself would have been a sham and none of those women would ever have gone to jail where they belonged.

He opened the first of the well-worn black books. He found the name he was looking for—a Senator who'd been elevated to the inner circle of the new President. A man who was spreading vicious rumors, hoping to ease Harris out of the job he intended to keep for life.

He dialed the Senator's home phone number. A quiet conversation before he read an entry or two about the Senator's past indiscretions. The silence at the other end soon led to an unspoken agreement. There would no longer be any restrictions on those wiretaps Harris knew were necessary for national security. He hung up the phone and smiled at Clint.

"Works like a charm every time." He unlocked the drawer and put the small black book on top of the two others.

Clint poured two glasses of Old Grand Dad. "To our long and prosperous future."

2.

THERE were days Daniel couldn't believe his own luck, but he knew better than to crow about it. Especially in front of Mattie's momma. That old lady saw sin sneaking into the house if you weren't always standing guard to keep it out. Daniel was afraid she'd turn their daughter into Bible-thumping Baptist when she grew up, but Mattie was more afraid her momma wouldn't live long enough to see their little girl grow.

Only it wasn't just luck that sent him to the Franklin Institute early that Saturday night. Once he heard about the raid Sergeant Callan was planning, Daniel knew he needed to warn Mattie. It might cost him his job, but he didn't care. He only worried he might not catch her in time.

And there she was—on her way to the store to pick up a few extra bottles of ginger ale for the party. He stopped her on the sidewalk and told her she was in grave danger of being surreptitiously apprehended. When she blinked and smiled at him, he was sure he was in love with her.

"The way you throw around big words like that, you could hurt yourself."

Somehow, she could tease him and still be kind.

"What I'm trying to say is you shouldn't go back there," he said.

"And you shouldn't go telling people what they should do," Mattie said.

A light rain started to fall at the same time dusk rose up. He led her under an awning to keep her from getting wet and tried to explain more plainly. There was going to be a raid.

"Then you're in just as much trouble as I am," she said. "Aren't you aiding and abetting a criminal?"

"I guess I am," he said.

Once Daniel started talking, it was hard for him to stop. There were so many conversations he'd been waiting to have with someone. And she was so easy to talk to.

It turned out they liked the same radio plays. The same kind of music. He hadn't been to the movies much, but he'd always wanted to go. It was funny how they kept on talking, neither one of them willing to step out from under the awning until Daniel saw two police cars coming down the block.

He wanted to see her safely home, he said, but Mattie said it looked like the only home she had any more was back in Smyrna, Tennessee.

Between the two of them, they had just enough money for bus fare and two cups of coffee. On the long ride South, they got to know each other so well, it seemed only natural to head straight to the justice of the peace when they arrived in Smyrna.

The first thing Daniel did when they moved into the white clapboard house with Mattie's momma was fix the hot water heater.

$$3.$$

ANDREW'S leg only bothered him when he walked up stairs. He leaned on his cane as he took the white marble steps slowly. His knee stiffened and ached, but it was worth all the pain to see Abraham Lincoln still sitting there. Still hopeful. The war hadn't changed him even if it seemed to Andrew it changed everything else.

Emily, who wrote weekly to swear she would wait for him until the end of time, ran out of patience in June and married someone on her father's staff. Lorraine stayed faithful, though he'd given her no reason to believe he had any intention of returning home to her. He was glad now she did. He was finally ready to go back to Muskegon, get married, and settle down to practicing law, which is what he should have done in the first place. They planned their wedding for the Saturday after Thanksgiving. John and his wife insisted he keep his promise to have the holiday meal at their house before he did anything else.

He took one last look around Washington. It seemed like more than a lifetime ago when he lived there. The city had grown bigger and more crowded, more impossible. It never did fit him right.

What's going to happen to this strange town now? Andrew asked Lincoln.

Lincoln, silent as a sphinx, gazed out to the middle distance.

About the Author and the book

You can learn more about C.P. Stiles and Washington in the 1940s at thecallhouse.com